For Mum, Dad and Keith

Also available by Karen Banfield

A Little Crime at Bedtime – a short story collection

Murder Around the Clock (Interactive version) – a murder mystery play. Published by Lazy Bee Scripts

Performances of full length Plays:

Murder is Addressed at Dembe Theatre, Tring and Limelight Theatre, Aylesbury in March 2025

A further Murder Mystery is scheduled for March 2026

The Conman with a Conscience – a play about money and morals at the Limelight Theatre, Aylesbury in October 2025

Fourteen Full length Murder Mystery plays available for performance, enquiries to Karen.banfield67@gmail.com

https://www.facebook.com/KarenBanfieldWriter

A Touch of Drama at Bedtime

a Short Story Collection

Karen Banfield

First published in 2024

by Banfield Publishing

All rights reserved

© Karen Banfield 2024

The moral right of Karen Banfield to be identified as the author of this work has been asserted by her in accordance with Section 77 of the Copyright, Designs and Patents Act 1988

This book is sold subject to the condition that it shall not, by way of trade or otherwise, be lent, re-sold, hired out or otherwise circulated without the author's prior consent in any form of binding or cover other than that in which it is published and without a similar condition including this condition being imposed on the subsequent purchaser.

This book is a work of fiction. Names, characters and incidents are the product of the author's imagination. Any resemblance to actual events or persons living, or dead, is coincidental.

Printed in Great Britain by Amazon

Cover design by Emma Tuohy via Canva and AI

ISBN: 9798300701437

Contents

Best Mum in the World	1
What Friends are For	5
What goes Around	9
The Gamble	19
The Empty House	27
Fair's Fair	33
Stroke of Luck	41
Love Thy Neighbour	45
Where Did She Go	53
The Journey from Paddington	57
The Birthday Surprise	63
Other People's Children	69
Homemaker	73
The Eighty Pound Rule	77
The Extra Plate	81
Off My Trolley	85
Things We Do for Love	93
Bachelor Boy	101
The Promise	109
The Cake Box	113
Half Full, Half Empty	117
Perfect Audience	119
Taking Notice	123
Matching Pair	127
The iPhone's Fault	133
A Nice Slice of Cake	135

Best Mum in the World *(Mark's Tale)*

I didn't realise what had really gone on, until I turned ten. I knew Mum was kind, because she cuddled me when I was upset and looked after me, but as far as I was concerned, it was her fault my dad had left. He'd said it over and over again, that if she didn't stop nagging him, he'd be off. Then one day, he wasn't home when I came back from school. After a while, Mum said he'd had to go away for work. He'd never had a job before, so I didn't believe her. She'd made it up because he'd left when he'd had enough of her going on at him. At first, I hated her, but that just wore me out, so I calmed down to just not liking her anymore.

It was Aunty Maxine that put me straight. She wasn't actually related to me, she was our next door neighbour, but back in the '70s that's what you called one of your mum's friends. She sat me down and said she'd had enough of standing by, hearing me complaining to Mum about going without. And, she was fed up of watching her struggle on when I should be helping her.

'But it's all her fault we haven't got any money. We would have if she hadn't driven Dad away with her nagging.' I said.

Aunty told me that wasn't the real reason he left. He hadn't even gone of his own free will, he'd been carted off to prison. The nagging my mother had done before he'd left, was to try and get him to find a proper job and stop burgling people's houses.

I could feel tears pricking my eyes, so I ran off, down the road thinking that it couldn't be true. Not my dad. I came home really late that night and I could tell that Mum was worried, but I didn't care.

'If your dad was here, he'd give you a good hiding,' she said.

I shouted at her, 'well he can't can he, if he's in prison.' I'm not sure who was most surprised, her or me.

'Who told you? Is it going all round school?' Her face went pale.

'No. Aunty Maxine did.'

She came and sat on my bed after I'd just climbed in and told me some home truths about Dad. He'd still got another three years to do. I cried that night and every night for the rest of the week. At the time I didn't know why it upset me so much. Now I can see that I was coming to terms with realising everything I'd thought about the two most important people in my life, was all wrong. I'd been wrong and given Mum a hard time, when all along, she'd only ever done her best. Guilt is a big burden for a ten-year-old. Luckily I soon realised the best way to get rid of it, was to be a better son to her and appreciate her a bit more. I think that's when I really started to grow up.

I didn't normally go to any events at school. The PTA always organised an annual fireworks display, but I just told the other kids I didn't fancy going, when in reality we couldn't afford it. But this year, the school was celebrating being 100 and there was to be this big event on Bonfire Night to make a thing of it. There was going to be some fairground stalls brought in, as well as hot dogs for sale and the big firework display. Everyone was talking about it and even the Dooley kids were going and there were so many of them, they never went anywhere. I thought it best Mum didn't know about it, otherwise she'd feel bad for me.

I'd begun to realise exactly how difficult Mum's life really was. We were known as a broken home, which was bad enough. Thank goodness everyone thought Dad had just run off and left us. Mum said the shame of everyone knowing he was inside, would have been unbearable. She didn't have any close friends apart from Aunty Maxine, everyone else had given her a wide berth once she was on her own, fearful she would entice their men from them. I saw more than one man put their arm around her, uninvited, so she had to smack their hands away. Although she worked full time in the factory, she didn't get paid what a man would have done. She was expected to be grateful they gave her a job at all.

Mum was great at getting bargains and saving up her Green Shield stamps. This year she needed to get a proper winter coat, because her rain-mac was so thin and my shoes were getting a bit tight, as well as Christmas being not far off.

I didn't know she'd got to hear about the big event, until one day she came home from work, all pleased. She handed over a ticket, warning me I mustn't lose it. I was so thrilled at first and then I started worrying.

'But we can't afford it' I said.

'Don't you worry about that. You just enjoy yourself. You deserve it.' And she kissed me on the top of my head.

I stood there in awe as the fireworks were set off, one after the other. It was so much better than watching from my bedroom window. Even now, fifty years later, I think of her and all her sacrifices, whenever I see fireworks.

When I'd pressed her as to where the money had come from for the ticket, she said she'd realised she didn't need a new coat after all. She'd just added some padding inside the lining of her rain-mac and it had worked a treat.

'What with?' I'd asked.

And she'd smiled at her own ingenuity. 'Newspaper.'

We both laughed as she moved her arms around and it crackled. That's how I remember her, best mum in the world.

What Friends are For *(Lisa's Tale)*

I hadn't heard from Nicole for ages, so I was surprised to get her call. After the usual catching up, she got round to the real reason for ringing me.

'Lisa,' she started nervously 'You know how you helped Debs out when her boyfriend had messed her about?'

'Yes,' I replied, smiling. 'She felt much better after we'd got a bit of revenge. So what's yours been up to?'

'Charlie and I have split up now, and I'm not sad to see the back of him. But when we were together, I let him borrow my car a few times, and now I've had two parking penalties come through. I rang them to explain I wasn't driving, but they weren't interested. I'm sure I could fight them, but I haven't the energy. Then they said if I didn't pay, eventually the bailiffs would come round.'

'That sounds scary. And I take it Charlie has declined to compensate you for his misdemeanours?'

'Exactly. That's a hundred and sixty quid.'

'I can lend you that if you need it.'

'That's so kind of you, but I'll be okay. It's the principle as much as anything. No, what I'd like you to do is teach him a lesson. Where it hurts him most, in his wallet.'

'Sounds like fun,' I said, picking up a pen. 'Tell me all about him.'

So here I am two weeks later, attending my first antiques auction. I'd gone to the viewing session yesterday and had a look at the lots. But today, there was a definite excitement in the air. There was a mixture of hardened traders and wide-eyed first timers like me. I heard a couple argue about whether or not the table and chairs were too big for their house and a man tell his partner that the painting was terrible and he wouldn't have it on any of their walls, except maybe in the garage. I bought a catalogue for two pounds and filled out the registration form to be given a bidding card.

I'd dressed carefully this morning, with my long brown wig, fake glasses with the black frames and my black coat; I looked very ordinary. Every time I'd been on stage with my different amateur dramatic groups, I acquired more bits of costume and it was times like this when they came in very handy.

I recognised Charlie from his Facebook page. Nicole had given me loads of details about Charlie's business, although that's really too grand a description, for what was really only a market stall. She'd said he particularly likes the first batch of stock that's auctioned at this place, because as well as individual items, there were boxes of mixed china and metal objects. This was where he often found his treasures, as he liked to describe them to his customers.

The catalogue gave a short description of what each lot contained. From Nicole's information, I underlined which ones Charlie was likely to bid on. The first few items went through fairly quickly and I was surprised with the speed at which it all happened. I waited for the hammer to come down dramatically and maybe a loud 'sold', but the auctioneer just tapped the tip of his pen against his clipboard and carried on. All of a sudden it was the first one I'd underlined and I started to feel nervous.

'Lot twenty-four, collection of mixed pottery, shall we say twenty pounds, anyone?' The auctioneer looked around the room, but no one moved.

'Ten then? Okay, eight pounds do I hear?'

Charlie held up his bidding card.

'Thank you that's eight then, ten I'll take.'

I held up my card and the auctioneer nodded at me.

'Thank you, ten, so twelve?'

Charlie held up his card again and glanced behind him to see who his rival was.

'Thank you twelve, I'll take fifteen'

I moved to be more hidden by the woman next to me and held up my card.

'Right, eighteen anyone?'

Charlie bid again. I decided, that was enough for my first time and shook my head when the auctioneer looked back at me.

'That's eighteen then, any more? No, right I'm selling at eighteen pounds.'

It was another thirty or so lots before I thought he'd bid again. He'd half-heartedly bid on something in between, but backed down long before the big money was pledged. The next one I'd picked out, had a higher estimate than some of the others, but when I'd looked through the box yesterday, there was a lot there that you could sell on a market stall. Apparently Charlie wasn't very well informed about the value and age of these sorts of things, but he could judge quite well what he could sell something for. As expected, Charlie was bidding, as were two others, so I stood back and watched for a while. When one of the others dropped out, I joined in.

Nicole had told me, that when it got down to just Charlie and one other bidder, he would often go way over what he wanted to, just to get the satisfaction of being the winner. We were up to sixty-eight now and it was just Charlie and I. He kept glancing over at me, but I knew I was quite well hidden in the crowd. I hadn't wanted to bid over eighty for this one, as it was going to take a bit of effort for me to resell the individual items on eBay if I ended up with it, but I was having such fun, I found myself going up to ninety. I let him have it at ninety-two pounds and grinned to myself over the victory of having pushed up the price he'd had to pay.

I stayed there for another hour, when I'd reached my goal. I'd worked out that, including the premium that went to the auction house, he'd paid two-hundred pounds more than if I hadn't bid as well.

It wasn't entirely satisfactory though as Nicole was still out of pocket. But I wasn't finished with him yet.

It was a light drizzle when I was standing, in my blonde wig and smart suit at his market stall, holding a small navy-blue vase with painted flowers. I'd bought it for one pound fifty in a charity shop.

Using my poshest voice, I said 'You sold this to my mother last month, telling her it was Moorcroft and therefore a snip at one hundred and sixty pounds. This is most certainly not Moorcroft and I demand the money back.'

He looked at me, taken aback as if no one had questioned his merchandise before. After a minute he said, 'I don't remember selling it. And if I did, I'd never say it was Moorcroft. The old girl must be confused.'

'There is nothing wrong with my mother. Now, either you give me a refund right now, or I write to the council suggesting they take away your permit for this market as you are making fraudulent statements about your goods.'

I'd specially chosen the Harpenden market to visit, because he'd been on their waiting list for a long time and it was now one of his most lucrative sites. I was quite sure he wouldn't want to do anything to jeopardise that.

'Well I don't give refunds. She can exchange it for something else.'

'Fraud is a very serious matter. Perhaps I shouldn't let it be just a council matter, perhaps the police should be called.' I got my mobile phone out of my pocket.

'All right, all right. Have your bleedin' money and tell her not to come back.' He snatched the vase from me and handed over the notes.

'Thank you.' I said haughtily and calmly walked away. Nicole was going to be very pleased.

What Goes Around *(Fiona's Tale)*

Some people make a greater impact on you than others and Ernest Haydon, was just such a man. From the moment he moved into the complex, he challenged me at every turn. I'd never known a resident like it. It started with the afternoon activities.

'Why do you do bingo?' He asked, slightly stooped as he leaned on his walking stick.

'The residents like it.' I answered, curious as to why he was asking. 'Catherine always says that Wednesday afternoons are the highlight of her week.'

'That's because it's for women. Everything you do here is for women.' He stared straight at me with his startling blue eyes.

'Of course it isn't. Men play as well, they can join in all the activities here.'

'I've not noticed any men at the Knit 'n' Natter sessions, and I think you'll agree that's because it's mostly considered a ladies' pastime.'

'Well, I suppose more women are drawn to join in with that, than men.'

'Has there in fact, ever been a man there?'

'No. There hasn't. You can't count Jonathan. When he turned up he was already getting very confused and thought it was where he was supposed to wait to be taken home. Apparently he thought he was at his grandma's house and she was having friends around.'

'So, we're agreed then, there isn't anything for the men, on a Thursday.'

'If you want to suggest an additional activity, you are very welcome to do so.' I answered hoping he would stop pestering me and give up on the idea. I had the monthly financial report to send in and I hated it at the best of times. Today I was even further behind than I normally was and just didn't have the patience for Ernest.

'Right, I'll do just that.' And he walked away, Lulu at his heels, wagging her tail.

The next day, he stopped me on my way back to the office and simply said, 'Poker.'

'Pardon?' I replied, taken aback.

'Thursday afternoons, we should have a poker game. For the ladies as well as the men, of course. We wouldn't want there to be any discrimination.' He looked pleased with himself.

'That's gambling, we can't have that.'

'No different to bingo. We don't have to play for money, just for a small prize. So what's the difference?'

'Well ...' I was at a loss as to what to say. When he put it like that, I suppose they're not so different. I didn't think it would go down very well with the other residents though. 'I'll have to see what everyone else thinks. I'll put a notice up on the board in the lounge.'

'Thank you kindly. I think starting next week would give plenty of time for word to get around.'

I left him, hoping the lack of interest from the others would keep him quiet. I hoped he wouldn't be too disappointed, as after all, he meant well. I'd tried all sorts in the past without getting much response.

I was therefore very surprised that every single male resident said they wanted the poker game. Even Bob who couldn't really follow a television programme any more, was apparently keen and suggested Texas Hold 'Em was the best choice for a group. Bob actually said Texas Hold On To Them, but corrected himself twice before settling on the correct name. And so I had no choice but to let them have a go. I even had to stand up for them when I next went in to Nationwide. The cashier moaned because Ernest had wanted his five-pound note changed into pennies for them to use as chips. Before I knew it I found myself saying 'Well the men need activities more suited to them than just knitting you know.' And to give Ernest his due, the poker game was as well attended as the knitting was. There were even a couple of women who played. Mind you, the men seemed rather grumpy whenever they won.

Having had a few run-ins with Ernest, I came to the conclusion that he must have been a barrister or a trade union rep during his working life. He was very articulate and whenever he wanted something, he put across his point very well. And most of the time he got his way. But even with the most persuasive words, he still couldn't achieve what he wanted for his one of his poker friends.

Reg's very elderly cat finally fell asleep for the last time and Ernest wanted permission for him to get another one. He said Marmite had been such good company for Reg and he didn't need to get a kitten or anything difficult to handle. But I had to be firm and remind him of the rules. Residents were allowed to bring a pet with them when they joined us, but they weren't allowed to replace them once they had gone. It was not a popular policy, and all I could repeat was that it was always made perfectly clear when anyone moved in. Ernest argued every time I saw him, that it wasn't fair and one more cat wasn't going to make any difference. I secretly agreed with him, but I didn't have the authority to go against the rules. Head office would have sacked me for sure if I did that. They weren't very happy about the poker sessions as it was.

I saw Ernest take a special interest in Reg after that, arranging DVD nights in each other's flats and going down the library together to choose their next one. He let Reg take Lulu out sometimes too and I could see how Reg perked up with these acts of kindness. Lulu certainly seemed to enjoy all the attention. I admired Ernest for letting his beloved dog out of his sight as I could see how anxious he was, looking out of the patio doors that faced onto the garden and the path that led round the corner to the front door. He virtually leapt out of his seat to greet them both when they returned and took Lulu's lead off Reg.

'Have a nice walk?' I'd hear him ask and then take Lulu back to his flat almost without waiting for an answer.

I next butted heads with Ernest over the décor in the lounge. It had been a few years since it was last decorated and so I'd been given a budget by head office to get someone in to wallpaper it and repaint the ceiling and woodwork. I had been to Homebase to get some samples and made the mistake of bringing them into the lounge when Ernest was in. I knew I should have waited for him to go out, but I was too keen to see what would look best.

'Ah, we're being made over are we?' He said as took one of the samples from me. 'Bit flowery.'

'Pretty though,' I answered.

'Let's have a look at that one.' He took another from me.

'Too flowery,' he pronounced. 'Next.'

I handed him the third sample.

'Still too flowery. None of these are right.'

'I'm following head office guidelines.' I replied.

'And what does that say exactly?' he asked.

'I'm to choose something that will provide a relaxing environment and be pleasing to the eye. It says something else like, flowers are particularly popular with residents and help bring the outside into the room. Then something about this helping the less mobile residents still feel close to nature.' I knew the policy quite well because I'd read it through a few times before I'd gone to Homebase. I had to be so careful not to go against them, I loved working here, with everyone and I'd be devastated if I lost my job. I'd heard my predecessor was sacked for allowing smoking in the covered area of the garden.

'We need something a bit different. A bolder, feature wall maybe and then plain colour for the other three, to accentuate the focal point.'

I pointed to the first one he looked at. 'That would be nice and bold'

'We want something more modern, something swirly maybe or geometric.'

'That won't make anyone feel close to nature.' I replied.

'No. No, that's true.' He looked thoughtful. 'Leave it with me will you, don't go buying any just yet.'

'All right,' I answered. It wasn't long before he came back to me. He was positively beaming with excitement.

'Photography club. That's what we'll set up. I've got a nice digital camera and the others can all use it to take photos or on their smartphones if they've got them.'

'Of what?'

'Nature of course. Those that can't go far can do the flowers in the garden and the rest can go out and about. We could share a taxi up to Stockgrove Country Park maybe, there's always squirrels there and the ducks on the lake of course. Then we can take them to Boots to get printed and put them up either side of the patio doors.'

'Won't that be expensive?'

'No. We'll only get the good ones printed and we can get some of those glass clip-on frames that aren't too dear.'

'I've never heard anyone say they were interested in taking photographs.' I muttered, thinking this was all getting rather out of hand.

'It can be a new group we could set up. Some of the guys would love that.' He looked directly at me, 'and the ladies too.'

'Do we need another club?' I asked. 'Over the last few months you've got poker going, the DVD nights you started with Reg that turned into big screen film nights, then there's curry night on Fridays.'

'Well who doesn't like a takeaway? And when you do a big order you can choose a bit from different dishes.'

'Yes I know, I've enjoyed joining in a couple of times. And by the way, there's talk of alternating with Chinese I heard. Mavis wants to try seaweed.'

'Good idea. And I'm trying to get a few more to join the book group. Five is okay, but we'd have more discussion if we had a few others.'

'There you go. That's all these different things you've set up. Surely we don't need a photography club as well.'

'We can see what people think, can't we? It's not me I'm thinking of. I can get out and about and enjoy the wildlife when I'm out with Lulu. Not everyone can do so much. But if they can get into the garden there are lots of flowers there to capture. Hey,' his face lighting up, 'we could have some photos of the pets as well.'

'Honestly Ernest, why do you keep doing so much?'

'Because the others like it. No, actually that's not it. They need it. When I came here, everyone was friendly, but apart from bingo and Knit 'n' Natter, there wasn't much going on. So a few came in here for a chat if anyone else was around, but otherwise it was pretty much deserted. People were staying in their flats, not really seeing anyone except you and only then if they needed your help with a problem. Their quality of life just wasn't as good as it could be. And when you've not got so many years left, you need to make every day count, not just quietly biding your time.'

'I'm sorry I can't spend more time with everyone. What with all the paperwork head office need me to do every day, writing down every little detail of this that or the other, how many times any of the residents have needed an ambulance, have I got reliable people coming in to offer hairdressing and chiropody, when did I get the fire extinguishers last checked. I tell you, it's never ending.' And to my horror I broke into tears. He put his arm round my shoulder and guided me into one of the high wing-back chairs. He even handed me a tissue. I blew my nose and took a deep breath. 'Thank you. I'm sorry about that.'

'Sounds like they work you too hard.' He said kindly.

'I try to do my best for the residents, I really do. I know I should have put on more activities. I tried last year to set up a Scrabble afternoon, but no one came. And then I did invite a speaker in to do a talk one Sunday on beekeeping. I thought that would be interesting, but only a few turned up for that as well.'

'Fiona, I'm not for a minute suggesting you haven't done as much as possible. These things are too much for someone in your position to sort out. You have so many other responsibilities, you can't be expected to put in the work it takes to enthuse and organise everyone. I haven't counted the hours I've been round knocking on doors, putting little notes through reminding people. Getting people to pair up with whoever they are most friendly with and agree to go together to things, until they get more confident. Old people get stuck in their ways, that's all. You just need to give them a prod sometimes.'

'Well you've certainly done that. I've heard nothing but good words for what you've achieved. I heard Reg whistling the other day. I hadn't realised he'd stopped after he lost Marmite, until I heard him again. Still out of tune mind you.'

'I like to help people. Always have.' He said.

'Was that what you did for a living then? Something that made a difference?'

'Well in a way. I ran the family dry cleaning business. People walked the streets of Leighton Buzzard in snow-white shirts, thanks to me.'

'But not problem solving?' I was really surprised.

'Not if you don't count getting red wine and fruit juice off of tablecloths, no.'

'You've missed your vocation then,' I said.

'Maybe. But there's always something you can do in life that can make a difference, even a small one. And I know if I needed anything, I'd have friends I could turn to. I'm a firm believer in what goes around, comes around.'

'So what about this wallpaper then? Do you want to get some samples of what you had in mind?'

'Yes. I'll do just that and we can Blu Tac them up in here and get some votes going.' He squeezed my hand as he stood up.

We now have a very interesting turquoise wall at one end with spiral patterns and cream for the rest of the room. The money I saved on wallpapering those, went towards the photo frames of the nature and pet pictures that are either side of the patio doors. The photography club have now moved to fortnightly gatherings as they said monthly was too long to wait.

But three months ago, the unthinkable happened. While out at the shop for his morning paper, there was an almighty crash as a car came up the kerb and hit a lamppost. Ernest was only a few feet away and in the uproar that followed, Lulu slipped out of her lead and ran off. He didn't notice at first, being shaken up by the near miss. The newsagent got a chair for him and offered him a hot drink. By the time he'd recovered from the shock, Lulu was nowhere to be seen. I helped him walk up and down the High Street, asking everyone we passed. I took one of the photographs of her from the lounge wall, had it enlarged, then copied onto posters that

I put up everywhere I could think of. The face of the West Highland Terrier peered at you from every direction within half a mile of the centre. The residents had even clubbed together to offer a small reward for her return.

I couldn't believe the change in Ernest after that. I told him the Fish and Chip van was planning to come on Fridays instead of Tuesdays and so it would clash with takeaway night, but he just said, people will just have to decide for themselves what they wanted. He closed his door and stayed in his flat. Nearly every resident must have knocked on his door since then, asking him to come to one of the clubs, or to join them for a cup of tea, but he politely refused. At first he went out all day, walking the streets to try and find her, but even that's stopped now.

I knew I had to do something. So here I am standing outside Ernest's door, hoping he won't be much longer as my arms were starting to ache. At last he stood in front of me and looked surprised at the bundle I was holding. The dog was smaller than Lulu, still a puppy really and desperate to be put down so it could explore.

'What are you doing with that?' he finally asked.

'She's yours,' I said

'That's not Lulu, you know it's not.'

'Of course it is. It's a Westie. Lulu's a Westie. Stands to reason she's yours.' I held the dog out and dropped her into his arms before he'd worked out what I was going to do. 'It couldn't be a new dog, because the rules don't allow anyone to replace a pet, so it's not new. It's Lulu.'

The dog started licking Ernest's face and for the first time in weeks he smiled.

'What if Lulu comes back?'

'We'll worry about that if it happens.'

He nodded. 'She was a lovely dog.'

I drew in a breath and said sternly 'I don't know what you mean Ernest, saying she was a lovely dog. She is a lovely dog, the one you're holding.'

He stared at me and then down at the lively animal that had taken an instant shine to him.

'Thank you.' He managed. As he bent down to let the dog explore his living room he looked up at me. 'Please call me Ernie. All my special friends do.'

The Gamble *(Emily's Tale)*

I tell myself I couldn't have known. But could I? I knew my sister better than anyone else in the world. Why then, couldn't I even consider the potential consequences, when I made that phone call? I took a big risk and it didn't pay off, so I have to do penance every day.

Marissa was six years younger than me and she'd been my living, adorable doll to play with, right from the start. Our mum was lovely, such a softy that the pair of us could wrap her round our little fingers. The trouble was, so could every employer she ever had, which meant she worked extra hours all the time, running errands way beyond her job description. She did her very best for us, we both knew that, but she was so tired when she came home, we learnt to be self-sufficient from an early age. Our father had walked out shortly after Marissa was born and hadn't been seen since. I don't think mum was surprised or particularly upset, she always described him as a free spirit and he couldn't bear to stay in one place too long. She said moving house was all right at first, but after the fourth time in as many years, he was ready to move again. But this time she'd refused, saying it was different now that I needed to go to school. So he made the move without us. She said she didn't really mind and was mildly nostalgic when a payment went into her bank account from him, out of the blue and a sometimes a postcard from somewhere remote. She said everyone was happier to be doing their own thing and gave us an extra hug.

When Mum was diagnosed, we all clung together, being even more united than before. We didn't know where Dad was, but we did try to ring him, but he must have changed his number as it was unobtainable. We all agreed he wouldn't be much use on parent duty anyway. And besides, I was seventeen and if mum could just hold out another three months, I'd be an adult myself and able to take care of Marissa. And bless Mum, she did just that, much to the surprise of the doctors and nurses who had made gloomy predictions of her only having at best, a few short weeks. The last thing any of us wanted was for social services to take

Marissa away from me, shoving her into a home and me to some hostel for the short time until I could fend for myself. It was the day after my birthday, that Mum slipped away in her sleep.

I sorted all the arrangements out, determined that I could prove to the world that I was in control and Marissa was safe in my care. I made sure she went to school every day and had clean uniform to wear, breakfast inside her, credit on her school lunch account and the correct PE kit on the right day. I took over Mum's old jobs, cleaning big houses for rich people. They were sympathetic to me, but still made a fuss if I missed a cobweb or forgot to empty the bin in the spare room. I knew I needed the money and so I smiled, apologised and got on with it as best I could.

Originally I intended to go to uni and learn business studies. I didn't really know what that was, but it was obviously going to lead to something in an office, which suited me as I was not an outdoors person, and I wasn't a lover of manual work. So the cleaning wasn't my first choice, but it wasn't so terrible that I wanted to give up the flexibility it offered me. When I finished for the day, I could be home by four o'clock to greet Marissa, which made it all worthwhile.

She wanted to go to uni too, so we looked at courses together when the time was right and found student loans and bursaries to pay for us to both go. We chose the most local so that we could continue living at home. Those were such good times. No more cleaning and spending more time with my sister. I'd watch her sometimes from across the kitchen table as she worked on her assignments, so proud of the confident girl she'd grown into. I knew Mum had done most of the work, but I secretly felt proud of my involvement in the process.

I don't know if it was because I had the responsibility of looking after her or not, but I never had much interest in boys. There were a few who were clearly interested in me, and I think that was all I needed. I was flattered enough to believe myself attractive, but not so drawn to anyone that I had to sacrifice my responsibilities. Marissa couldn't be more different. She usually had boys buzzing around her all the time, in little groups, vying for position to edge their way as close to her as possible. But she never stayed with anyone for very long, she was like a butterfly flitting from one to another. I asked her once why she never kept a boyfriend longer than two months and she said she liked the excitement of getting to know someone new, but once that had passed, she lost interest.

Mum had, of course, already explained to both of us where babies came from and whenever I asked Marissa if she was being sensible, she laughed at me and said of course she was. But something went wrong, as she began feeling tired and sick, soon to discover that she was pregnant. When I asked her who the father was, she confessed she wasn't sure. We wondered about testing the baby and the possible subjects, but she said she'd rather not as she wasn't with any of them anymore, so it would be awkward maintaining an ongoing relationship. We talked about her options but quickly dismissed the idea of getting rid of it and started to plan timetables so that we could both look after the baby. She was overjoyed when he arrived and she called him Theo. So, with history repeating itself, the Furston women just got on with it.

Marissa was a wonderful mother. That's why I did what I did. Because I knew that was the real her. She never got cross at being woken up several times a night and when he was going through the terrible-two's, she was calm but firm with him until he came out of it the other side. She didn't let him see her cry when she dropped him off for his first day at pre-school, she saved it until she was safely out of sight.

When he was six, Marissa was pregnant again. She knew who the father was this time, but he was married and she didn't see any point in telling him. She said how unlucky she was to have got caught when he was the only man she'd been with in the last six years, as her focus had been entirely on Theo. The married man had pursued her and charmed her into acting out of character. But she didn't mind the pregnancy, she said she loved Theo so much and he'd brought her so much joy, another baby would do the same. And how nice it would be to have a sibling. She looked at me and said, wasn't it funny, there would be the same gap between them as there was between her and I. The baby was a boy too, so they'd be same-sex siblings, just like us. I can still remember her expression, she was so happy.

In her eighth month, she went into labour. It happened quickly, but still with enough time to get to the hospital. But it didn't make a difference. Her beautiful baby wouldn't breathe and they pronounced him dead.

Over those dark days, neither Theo nor I could console her. She kept saying she wanted to be on her own. In the end, I agreed to take Theo and for us to stay with my friend Francesca. It was a bit of a drive to get him to and from school, but I was glad to help Marissa any way I could. The accounts office I'd now been working at for two years, was great, allowing me flexi-time and working from home to make up for finishing early.

We visited Marissa every weekend, but she wasn't herself. I told her to see the GP and see if she could have some antidepressants. Even without any medical training it was obvious what she was suffering from. But she said it wasn't, she was grieving. I told her I understood, but in truth I didn't fully. I completely misjudged the bond she'd had with the baby and the subsequent trauma of losing him.

I did call a bereavement counsellor, and she said that she was sure she could help. She said that it should never be underestimated, as to how devastating a stillbirth could be. She confirmed that, from what I described, Marissa definitely needed help. When I told her what they'd said, she just kept saying no one understood, and she didn't want to see anyone. It broke my heart when Theo showed her the picture he'd drawn for her, but she could only manage the shortest of glances at it and only the hint of a smile to him. She ruffled his hair as if he was a dog or someone else's child, not like he was her Theo that she'd been devoted to.

I rang her GP and asked him to make a home visit, making up a story about her having a terrible pain in her back that made it impossible for her to get down to the surgery. He suggested painkillers from over the counter and that if it got worse to call an ambulance, but I managed to persuade him that she absolutely needed him to see where her pain was and that she couldn't face the hospital if she didn't have to. I mentioned the stillbirth and that visiting a hospital would bring it all back. He agreed he'd come later that day and I stayed in with Marissa, work having been agreeable yet again. When he arrived, he wasn't very pleased to say the least, when he saw Marissa walking around clearly pain-free. I explained to him I was desperate for her to get help, but that she'd refused, and I couldn't think of any other way. He softened and offered to talk to her about how she was feeling. But she wouldn't cooperate and so he left with the platitude that she knew where he was if she changed her mind.

I was at my wits end. It wasn't that I minded looking after Theo, far from it. I loved him as if he was my own son, but he needed her. And although she couldn't see it, she needed him too. She just had to realise it. So I didn't have a choice, I had to take drastic action. What else could I do?

I told her I was going to take Theo to visit the dinosaur theme park at the weekend. He'd been wanting to go there for a while. We'd leave early to try and avoid too much traffic on the motorway. I felt a bit mean, because I wasn't really going to take him, but I resolved to do so on another day. When Marissa was more herself, we'd all go and enjoy it together. That would be even better for Theo. It felt like days had passed before it was finally late enough for me to ring her. I used my mobile and walked down to the main road, which was heavy with traffic. It would sound quite convincing as a motorway. She answered on the seventh ring. I spoke, putting panic into my voice and limited what I said.

'There's been an accident on the motorway, it's Theo. He's hurt. I'll ring you again when I know more.' Then I hung up on her. I expected her to ring back or to text me, begging for more details. Crucially, was her son badly hurt? But it was silent. I was so disappointed. She should have been jolted back into action. She should have been so shocked by the news that she realised what was important, who was important. I had planned to make a second call, just in case the first one didn't do the trick, but had hoped I wouldn't need it. I waited again.

I called, but again, she didn't pick up immediately. Why not? Why didn't she have it right next to her, beside herself with worry? She did ask me how he was. I said I was at the hospital and that they were taking him into theatre. And this is where I made the biggest mistake of my life. She asked me if he was going to pull through. I should have said yes, definitely, but that she should come now so that she'd be there when he woke up. Why didn't I say yes? I didn't say no, just that they'd said how poorly he was. I heard her sob and told her she needed to come to him. I started telling her which roads to go on to get to the hospital. I planned to drive Theo and me there, and be waiting for her. I was ready for her to be angry, furious even at my underhand tactics when she realised there had been no crash and he was fine. By then it wouldn't have mattered. She'd have found herself again and been Theo's mum once more. I could live with her wrath against me, if it reunited them.

She told me she couldn't come to the hospital. That she couldn't face losing another child in one of those places. She sobbed and sobbed that she couldn't bear it. That she couldn't go through that again. And then she hung up. I tried to call her back, but she'd switched it off. It went straight to voicemail. On the third attempt, I left a message for her to call me immediately. I said the doctors had said he was now going to be all right. He wasn't as badly hurt as they'd first thought. By the sixth message, I dropped the pretence entirely and came clean. I left Theo with Francesca and headed over to her house, but it was a thirty-minute drive and the traffic was against me.

I got there too late. I let myself in and there she was, on the kitchen floor with blood everywhere. The kitchen knife she'd used on her wrists was lying next to her. I checked her pulse and called an ambulance, but there was nothing they could do. I sat down on the floor, in her blood and howled. I was beyond sobbing and crying, I let out a primal scream that I would never have thought was in me. But then I never for a moment would have thought I would be responsible for killing my beloved sister.

The paramedics asked if someone could be with me, to support me. I said I'd ring someone, to get them off my back, knowing that I wouldn't make any such call. I didn't deserve support, I needed to feel this, all of it, because it was all my fault.

Theo adjusted well. I hoped I was doing a good job of bringing him up. I try to be the best mother I can, even when I'm tired or ill. I don't let myself take the easy way out by letting him play games on a tablet or the TV. I play with him and play, way beyond the point I'm bored with the game or should be able to relax and have some time for me. That's the way it is now. It's all about him. I have to make it up to him. Every day I question myself on whether I am making the right decisions over his care. Was I being too soft with him, indulgent and spoiling, or too strict? I go to bed every night with my worry and my guilt and know I deserve it all.

The Empty House *(Georgina's Tale)*

My nerves were on edge before I even entered the house. The newspaper stories of the seven knife attacks that had taken place over the past few weeks had made me feel really uneasy. I wished now that I hadn't bought that paper on impulse at the newsagents, before I got my train, but the journey is so repetitive that I felt beyond bored, being jolted around, every morning, every night. Not for the first time I wished my job as a chiropractor was suitable for working from home and that I could work normal office hours. I should have skipped the latest report on The Hooded Man. It wasn't even an original name, since most people robbing and burgling were men wearing dark hoodies.

This part of Hertfordshire had never known such violence. I think that's what made it worse. People had been relaxed before, women were cautious about walking alone at night, but there was never any real danger. Not like there was now.

I did not want to go back to the house that night, but I'd left my phone there. It was at the end of a row of four Victorian terraced houses. It was small, but it all belonged to Josh and me. We were not planning to move into it until we had put the new kitchen and bathroom in, so it would be several weeks or even months before that happened. We'd bought it at auction as somewhere needing to be completely updated. That's how we were just about able to afford it, along with some money Josh's Great Aunt Christine had left him. We only really had the weekends to work on it or on my day off in lieu if I worked a Saturday, since we both worked long hours and were so tired by the time we got home from work. Occasionally Josh would go there for an odd hour or so during the day, depending on what deliveries he had to make for the furniture company that employed him.

I could not think how I was so stupid as to not notice that my phone had fallen out of my handbag, it normally never left my sight. We were working through the rooms one at a time, and yesterday it had been the main bedroom we had worked on. We had found stripping umpteen layers of wallpaper had proved to be a much lengthier job than either of us had imagined. We didn't think it would be finished for three or four weeks, unless we were really lucky. We had joked that some of the wallpaper must have been put up when the house was first built, it was stuck so solidly.

It was not a cold night, but as I walked away from the railway station I felt a chill run through me. I pulled my new navy coat tightly around me. The wool fibres tickled my neck, but the irritation was not enough for me to give up the comfort the coat gave me. I'd mislaid my soft polka dot scarf, so that was another thing I needed to try and find. It had just gone eight o'clock and the streetlamps gave a dull yellow glow over the roads, which were still busy with people scurrying home. The heavy rain had stopped now, but the roads were very wet. As I hurried along I was concentrating on trying to locate my gloves in my pockets and didn't look where I was going. I stepped straight into the middle of a deep puddle and the sudden coldness made me cry out. A middle-aged man stopped beside me.

'Are you all right?' he asked as he moved closer to me.

'Y-yes thanks.' I stammered.

He took hold of my arm and I gasped as I pulled myself away from him.

'I'm sorry, I didn't mean to frighten you.' He said, 'I thought you were a bit unsteady.'

'No.' I replied sharply and then more kindly, 'I'm fine thank you.' I moved over to the wall and leaned against it. I looked down at my wet foot and tipped muddy-brown water out of my shoe. As I replaced it I noticed the man was still standing there, staring straight back at me.

'Well if you're sure, I'll leave you to it.' He said as he lifted his right hand in a kind of wave and started to walk away.

I breathed a sigh of relief and stood there a few moments to compose myself before moving on. I wished I was walking home now, to the flat we shared with my sister, just around the corner, but I knew I had to get the phone. Goodness knows how many missed texts and WhatsApp messages I'd missed.

I turned away from the main street down into Maybury Avenue, it was quieter there so I quickened my pace, eager to get to Wallace Drive. Soon there were no more people around, all the houses had their curtains pulled tightly shut. As I hurried on I tried to remember where I had left my handbag the previous day. The hallway seemed the most likely place where the phone would have fallen out of my bag. I was cheered up by the thought of where it should be.

As well as the tap-tapping of my shoes, I fancied I heard heavy footsteps behind me. I pulled my handbag round to the front of me, holding tightly on to it and walked faster. The footsteps seemed to quicken and the gap between us had got shorter. I glanced over my shoulder and just made out the dark-coated figure of a man. It reminded me of the one that had stopped to help me, or so he'd said that's what he was doing. But maybe he had been sussing me out.

I crossed over the road and broke into a run, darting down the next right turn into Wallace Drive and stopping at number forty-seven. Fumbling for my keys, I tried to get it into the lock as quickly as I could. My hands were trembling, and I started to panic that it wasn't working when I realised I was trying the wrong key. I hastily found the right one and turned it in the lock, my heart thumping as the door opened and I stepped inside. I slammed it shut behind me and sank to the floor. I took deep breaths and sat there for a few moments.
I felt safe now and began to feel that I had overreacted out there in the street. I almost laughed at myself.

The light in the hall didn't work, so I turned on the landing light. It helped a little, but not enough for me to see my phone anywhere.

I went upstairs, along the narrow landing towards the main bedroom that was at the back of the house. I groped around the door for the dimmer switch on the edge of the wall. In my eagerness to switch the light on, I twisted the dimmer too far around. The knob shot across the floor.

'Damn it.' I said, wishing again that I had my phone so that I could use the torch setting.

It was then that I first heard the noise. I could not quite make out what had been said, but I was positive it was an adult and not a child's voice. My body froze and I could not move or say anything. The second time I heard it, I understood what was said.

'Sssh,' he went.

At that instant I came to life. I reached down for the stick that we'd got ready to stir the paint and ran down the stairs with it, as if my life depended on it, for at that moment, I thought it did. He wasn't going to shush me.

But there he was, in the hallway. I didn't stop to think that he was somewhere different to where the noise had come from, I was too terrified. I raised my arm and hit him hard with the stick, knocking his glasses flying. I pushed past him to get to the front door that was partly open, but seeing his face stopped me in my tracks.

'Josh, oh my God are you all right?'

'Jesus that hurt. What did you do that for?'

'I thought you were The Hooded Man. Here, let me get your glasses.' I picked them up and handed them to him. 'Anyway, we can't stay here, he's upstairs.'

'He can't be.' Josh said rubbing the side of his face.

And then we both heard it.

'Ssssh.'

'It's him.' I shrieked, grabbing his arm, desperately trying to pull him out of the front door.

Instead of complying, he gently pulled away and started laughing. 'It's not a man. Come on I'll show you.'

He led me upstairs into the bedroom. I held the stick up, just in case. Josh turned on the torch on his phone and there was the culprit. This is what had frightened the life out of me.

'I was here earlier on today after I'd been to the DIY shop in the high street and bought something to make all this decorating a whole lot easier. That's why I've come back tonight, because I remembered I hadn't switched it off,' he explained. He looked at the confused expression on my face and continued, 'it's for stripping the wallpaper, it produces steam out of these jets and you just scrape the wet paper off the wall.'

Another 'ssssh' came from the corner of the room behind the rolls of wallpaper and I recognised it as the noise I'd heard before.

'I got that big patch done and I was only at it for ten minutes. Had to go up to Watford so I didn't have long.'

'Wow, that would have taken over an hour the way we had been doing it.' I was impressed, but still a bit too shaken to take it all in.

He leaned forward and switched it off at the wall. He put his arm around me and I laughed at my overactive imagination.

'Come on,' he said, 'let's go home.'

It was not until we were lying in bed that night, that Josh asked me what I had been doing in the house. That's when I remembered I still hadn't got my phone.

Fair's Fair *(Moira's Tale)*

My brother was definitely the favourite child. The youngest, and so the cutest. Dad just loved referring to him as "son" and they went off for the day for football or fishing or any number of other male-orientated activities, which I was never invited to. Mum was nice to me, but I knew I was a bit of a disappointment. She was fond of saying how much she loved us both the same and that she made sure we were treated the same. Except this was usually when she was treating Christopher better than I was. She made him the dinner that she knew was his favourite at least once a week. She wouldn't mind turning the TV over for him to watch any wildlife programme that David Attenborough was narrating, but, if I asked to see something on another channel, she'd make me wait until her programme was finished.

I'm not jealous of Christopher, I'm not petty like that. Mum and Dad always described him as the clever one and were delighted when he got accepted at university. They said I had other qualities when I didn't get very high marks in my GCSEs, although they never managed to say what those qualities actually were. I got a job at a clothing factory, stitching fancy clothes all day long, the likes of which I'd never have an occasion to wear.

I got a council flat to move to from Mum and Dad's house and I did all right. I had friends that I saw on Saturday nights and I stayed in bed most of Sundays. Sometimes waking up with a man I vaguely remembered from the night before, but more often on my own. I found having to accommodate someone else's needs more tiring than rewarding, so I didn't go looking for a partner very often.

Christopher had gone down a well-trodden career path of accountancy. He was now a partner in a small practice in our hometown, with his wife Letitia who he had met at university. And they had two boys that go to the grammar school, so a nice perfect life. But I wasn't jealous. I think it's very shallow, to be envious of someone's lifestyle.

I had to give up the flat after Mum had a nasty fall. Dad had long since passed away by then. She broke so many bones, she ended up with more metal in her than there was bone. When the arthritis got worse it was a case of someone living with her or her going into a care home. The neighbours where I lived had started to cause a real nuisance by then, playing loud music and having slanging matches at all hours. The lift never worked and even if it did, you couldn't trust it wouldn't leave you stuck between levels for hours, without anyone coming to help. Mum had a lovely house, and she was easy company, so I was quite happy.

I gave up working at the factory as well, as she couldn't get by all day on her own. I can't say I missed it. Some of the other girls had been a laugh, but I could still go out for a drink with them and keep up with all the gossip. When Dad died, Mum wrote a will, leaving everything to be split 50-50 between me and Christopher. She said that she wanted to treat us both the same. She loved us both the same. I thought to myself that whilst that might be true, she liked him better than she did me, that was for sure. I didn't mind about splitting everything half and half, as at that stage it would have been just a bonus to me.

It was after I moved in, that I started to think I should get a bit more. After all, I'd given up my flat to help her. And it was so different these days. I'd got mine in the first place by just being on the waiting list. Now you had to be half dead or have umpteen children to qualify. I worried I'd have nowhere to go when Mum finally popped her clogs.

To give Mum her due, when I mentioned this, she saw my point straight away. She rang Christopher, him being too busy to have the time to visit, and asked him if he minded her leaving the house all to me. He could have the investments she'd got, which were quite substantial as Dad had been in an employee share scheme all his working life and the value had rocketed over the years. He said of course he didn't mind. He appreciated what I was doing for Mum and it wouldn't be right for me to lose my home.

'I am pleased,' she'd said. 'Fair's fair. And I love you both the same.'

I was relieved about the house. If it had been sold and the proceeds split between us, I wouldn't have had enough to buy myself anything decent. Then I started to think about what I'd have to live off. Whilst Mum was around, I got benefits for caring for her, but if she died, I'd got no job to go back to. I'd never be able to work out the fancy machines they'd have in the factory now. I'd been away from it for too long. I began to think I deserved the investment money too. I thought Mum might see my point of view, just as she had with the house. But to my annoyance, she was shocked at the very idea. She said I was perfectly capable of finding another job and I could work as a carer, since I'd done so well looking after her.

I was not impressed with this suggestion at all. Caring for my dear old mother was one thing, especially if she was leaving me the house. Caring for some stranger was another thing entirely. I fumed quietly for days after we'd had that conversation. Mum didn't seem to notice and I didn't let it show how I really felt. I fleetingly considered if Christopher would give me the investment money of his own free will, but I dismissed this as soon as I'd thought it.

Mum and I lived a good life. She was still very sociable and so we went to various groups and outings. We liked the same detective programmes on the TV and so we were comfortable together, just like some old married couple. She didn't even need too much hands-on looking after as she tried hard to do as much for herself as she could. The blight to my happiness was the same that had existed throughout my life, my dear brother.

He hardly bothered to visit Mum, even though he only lived a couple of miles away. He rang quite frequently, but usually when he was driving along and using his fancy car's hands-free function. He didn't ask how she was doing, just boasting about his work and how many new clients he was taking on. I always knew when he'd rung her as she was a bit quieter and wanting her daily vodka and tonic earlier than usual. The grandsons didn't come to visit much either. She was so forgiving, saying how hard they'd have to work at the grammar school. Only clever boys got in there. They'd have hours and hours of homework to do each night. Of course they wouldn't have time to visit their old grandmother. I tried to say that they seemed to have time to play their computer games, since they always asked for more expensive ones for each birthday and Christmas, but she wasn't convinced.

I got myself a new phone a few months ago and started using Facebook for the first time. Mum has trouble with her eyes now, so she can't read the small screen anymore. I made online friends with all sorts of people and of course had Christopher, Letitia and my nephews on there too. Letitia was always busy with some do-gooding or other. Not visiting her mother-in-law, I thought. Mum liked me to read out all the posts, so she could keep up with what they were doing. But she didn't want me to tell Christopher I did this. She said she wanted him to think he was telling her news she didn't already know, so it didn't spoil it for him. I thought she was more likely to be worried he'd stop calling altogether if he knew she was keeping tabs on what he was up to.

It made me cross when I saw some posts about their expensive holidays abroad and the constant meals out that they had. They spent an awful lot of their time dining out or popping up to London to see the latest musical at the West End. They never offered to take Mum out for a fancy dinner or to see a show. She'd have loved that. She refused point-blank to spend any of Dad's investment money to treat herself, so we had to get by on the benefits we could both claim. It was manageable but not luxurious. Not the lifestyle Christopher was living, that was for sure.

The more Facebook posts I read of their lives, the angrier I became. I thought about how selfish he was and how unfair it was he'd get that money, when he clearly didn't need it. I was seething when he posted they'd gone skiing on the spur of the moment as they'd had such a busy time, they'd just had to get away. Busy my backside, I thought. They should try managing on a shoestring and having to run around after a disabled person all day long. They'd know what needing a break really felt like. I read the details out to Mum and she just said she was pleased for them, that Christopher always loved the snow and wished him well. I asked her if she wanted to go back to Butlins this year and she said yes, of course, they put on such good entertainment. Not as good as an après-ski party I thought.

I decided I couldn't stand by and watch Christopher get what should rightly be mine. I'd given up my job to look after Mum and I needed that money to live off until I got my own pension. He didn't deserve it. I chose not to raise it with Mum again as I knew she never coped well with direct confrontation. I'd have to work harder than that. I started by making up things they were supposed to have added to Facebook. It would be Mother's Day soon and Christopher usually made an appearance for half an hour. Long enough to drink the cup of tea I'd make for him and present her with a bunch of flowers he'd have bought from Tesco, or more likely that Letitia had. Mum treasured these visits, and I felt sorry for her, that he didn't care enough back, to bother coming round more often.

I told her he'd bought a brand new car and showed her a picture of a random car I'd pulled off a dealership website. It's a BMW convertible. She asked me how much I thought that would have set him back and I said about seventy or eighty thousand. She nearly choked on her vodka. I casually added that it reminded me I needed to renew my season ticket for the bus. I think that's what made her realise, the difference between what he had and what I'd have after she'd gone. She was quite frail now having reached a ripe old age.

There was a programme on the TV a few nights after that, doing a report on life in modern Britain and surviving on the minimum wage. Helpfully they mentioned the sort of workers who were paid this, including care workers. She said it was a disgrace they were paid so little. Well, I said, I suppose people can work overtime, if they're up to it after their 40 or 50 hour shifts. I left the room and let her ponder on that.

Not long after I'd lied about the car and the documentary had come on, she rang the solicitors she'd used before and got them to come round.

'I love you both the same,' she said, 'but Christopher doesn't need Dad's investments and you will dear.' And she was so pleased it added up to nearly twenty thousand pounds. She patted my hand in an unusually affectionate gesture.

'Thanks Mum,' I said.

She died not long after. Christopher came round to see if he could help sort things out. I felt I ought to broach the subject of the inheritance. I wasn't pleased Mum had died, I really wasn't. But she'd had a good long life. And I still thought it was fair I got it all, because I'd been the one to give up everything. I do confess to feeling delighted that I didn't have to share it or see all the money go to my annoying little brother. Fair's fair I thought. I did the work, I should have the reward.

I told him how Mum had been so concerned about how I'd get by day to day and that's why she left the money to me. I told him she'd always said she loved us both the same. He looked at me strangely and said maybe that was true for Mum, but he knew he'd been Dad's favourite and no that wasn't a good thing, it was a curse. I started to feel sorry for him when he went on about all the fishing trips he'd been dragged along to and how boring it had been. And the umpteen sports he'd had to get involved in.

It had been difficult when Dad had died, so suddenly, from a heart attack. He'd never talked about wills and what he'd leave to anyone, and we'd always assumed that everything would go to Mum. But he had left a collection to each of his children. Christopher had some coins, and I had his stamps, including some that were really rare. There were first-day covers too. It was at a time they were fairly valuable, so I sold them and had a lovely holiday to Thailand with the proceeds. I'd occasionally looked at stamp prices since and because they varied so much, I was happy I'd got a good price when I sold them.

I hoped that Christopher effectively getting nothing from Mum's will, wouldn't turn him against me. We didn't have much in common, but I suddenly felt more alone now that Mum had died. And family are supposed to be more loyal than friends and I didn't want any estrangement. I said he was welcome to take anything from the house, as a memento of Mum. He said he'd have the bookcase then, if I was sure and so we left it very amicably. I wasn't much of a reader so I didn't bother replacing it.

As he came back into the kitchen after it had been safely stowed in the back of his car, I asked him again if he was all right with Mum's will. I found I really didn't want to fall out with him and toyed with offering to share it. But then he said that he wasn't bothered, honestly as he'd not long ago sold the coin collection he'd inherited from Dad. They'd been worth enough to pay off their mortgage and redecorate. So fair's fair he said, we each got a house from them one way or another. I thought of his massive six-bed house with a garden so long you couldn't see the end of it and then of Mum's two-bedroom terrace. I wondered how much it would cost to repaint it, given that it hadn't seen a paintbrush since we were children. Probably most of my twenty thousand. It was not fair at all.

Stroke of Luck *(David's Tale)*

My counsellor would tell me I mustn't think like this. That what happens in life is either of our own making, or just normal things that are beyond our control. Not from luck, good or bad. But as I stood looking at the van parked outside Hayley's house, I couldn't think it was anything other than that. I came every year, on her birthday and put a card through her letterbox. I needed her to know I was thinking about her, that I loved her and that I was sorry I'd messed up so much in the past. But this year, a dentist visit made me come a day earlier than usual and if I hadn't, I'd have been too late.

I stood and watched the two young men bring furniture and boxes out and then before I knew it, she was there too. I thought I was too far back for her to notice me but I wasn't so distant that I couldn't see what a beautiful woman she was. From what I could tell from her body language, she seemed full of confidence, waving her arm as she seemed to give instructions. I smiled. I'd so nearly missed her and I had no idea how I would have tracked her down after that.

She looked in my direction, as if my smile had been movement enough for her to notice me. I looked down so she wouldn't recognise me. I wasn't ready to talk to her. I hadn't prepared for that, only to post the card. From the corner of my eye I saw her go back inside the house and I let out a breath, unaware that I'd been holding it in. I couldn't work out what to do next; go and ask one of the removal men where they were taking everything or man up and go and ask her myself. I didn't think the men would tell me, after all I was some scruffy middle-aged man that looked like he had no business following Hayley to her new home.

The longer I stood there, the more I could feel the panic rising. If I didn't do something soon, I'd lose her and this time for good. If I'd had a car, I would have followed them, hoping I was far enough back not to be spotted but close enough not to lose them. But the reason I didn't have a car was the same reason I'd lost Hayley in the first place.

The men carried a sofa out together and loaded it in the van, before disappearing inside the house again. I wondered if they might have some paperwork, maybe on the top of the dashboard, telling them of the new address. Perhaps I could look through the window and see if there was some clipboard with all the details. I walked swiftly over and stood at the side of the road, peering inside, hoping my luck would hold. There was a load of rubbish in the footwell and side pockets, but nothing official looking. The van was plain white, so there wasn't even a company name to ring, not that it was all that likely they'd tell me. But given a bit of time, maybe I could have come up with something plausible.

Before I had time to think of my next move, I heard an angry voice behind me.

'Oi, what do you think you're doing?' The eldest of the two men barked at me.

'Nothing,' I managed, taking a step back.

'There's nothing to nick here, clear off.' he said, moving closer to me.

'Ok, ok.' I turned around to walk back the way I'd come and that's when I came face to face with her.

'Oh my God. It is you!' she said.

I tucked my hands in my pockets and just stood there, frozen to the spot.

'Dad.' She said, but not angry as I was expecting.

'Hello love.' I managed, wanting nothing more than to throw my arms around her and beg for forgiveness, but I was too ashamed of myself to think I deserved any of that.

'Are you all right?' she asked.

I looked at her, taking in her features, her dark hair pushed behind her ears revealing the same cute nose and deep brown eyes that I'd loved looking at, many years ago. I felt as if I was on the edge of a cliff, that if I did the wrong thing now, it would all be over. I stood, paralysed only managing to open my mouth but not enough to say any words. I managed to nod.

'Where on earth have you been?' she said and put her arms around me.

I'm not one to believe in miracles but surely this was one. I'd let her down so badly, yet she seemed to be giving me another chance. I hugged her back and the tears just rolled down my cheeks. All the years of missing her, unleashed. After a few moments I managed to sob that I was sorry, so, so sorry. She took me by the hand and led me into the house, sitting me down on one of the last two dining chairs.

'Where are you moving to?' I managed, pushing aside what we really needed to talk about, what I needed to say, to apologise.

'Spain,' she answered, 'to join Luke, my boyfriend. He runs a bar out there.'

I felt a stab in my chest. 'Abroad,' was all I managed to say, still thinking I was lucky I had caught her at all, but that it had run out now and I was about to lose her again.

'Only for the summer. He's moving back in October. But what happened to you? Are you all right?'

I smiled at her and at her generous spirit. 'I'm doing better. Getting help and it works most of the time.'

'That's so great,' she said.

'But I can't forgive myself for what I did to you and your mum.'

'What?' She asked 'Leaving?'

'No. Gambling away the rent money. Spending every penny so that the electricity got cut off. Spending the money your mum put aside to buy you new school uniform.' I went on, listing time after time that I'd been so selfish, what I could only think of now as wickedness. Why hadn't I bothered to get help earlier? Why hadn't I been able to put my wife and lovely little girl first? I hung my head again, too ashamed to meet her gaze. Surely now I'd reminded her of my worst crimes, she'd push me away. There would be no more hugging.

'Oh Dad, none of that matters anymore.'

'Of course it matters. You must have minded and been furious at me. Hated my guts.'

'Well I did, but then I was a teenager. I was permanently furious and hated everyone. I doubt if I'd have been any different even if I had every luxury and present I demanded.'

'How's your mum?' I had a whole different lot of guilt for letting her down.

'She's okay actually. Obviously she was cross when you left. But you'd argued such a lot beforehand, in a way she was happier.'

'But homeless and penniless.'

'Well the landlord was really sweet. He let her catch up on the arrears over time and Mum got a job in Tesco, so she had money coming in. I mean it wasn't perfect but it wasn't terrible. She got promoted pretty soon and started seeing the bloke on the fish counter. I called him Stinky Pete, but actually he's really nice.'

'I thought you'd have been kicked out and put up in some bed and breakfast by the council. No car, because that had already been repossessed and no money.'

'Oh Dad, the worst bit was missing you. I got a birthday card from you but you never put on it where you were. And how did you find me anyway?'

'That was a stroke of luck too. I saw your picture in the paper, when the estate agents you worked for, got that award. I had one of the women from the gambling group follow you home one night. I made sure she knew not to get too close and scare you.'

'That is enterprising.'

'But why don't you hate me?'

'Because I've come to understand what addictions can be like. And Mum stuck up for you, saying it wasn't your fault. So I stopped caring about the material things. When I got a bit older, I let it all go. All that was left was that I needed my Dad. And now I've finally got you.' She put her arms around me again.

I was totally thrown by her reaction. To be given another chance was beyond my wildest dream. Even my counsellor couldn't deny it, as this really was my lucky day.

Love Thy Neighbour *(Alison's Tale)*

From the minute I arrived and introduced myself, I felt blessed to be living next door to the Thompsons. Tyler was an estate agent and Caitlin worked in a care home. They had a very friendly Labrador called Hamish and there was also Tyler's daughter Destiny, who came to stay on alternate weekends. I was so lucky because they let me share their lives. I think I would have been quite lonely otherwise, especially when I first moved here.

It had always been my choice to live on my own, but my days were usually rather quiet. I was self-employed as a bookkeeper and so I didn't see many people during the day. I preferred that and I think that's why I was drawn to it as a career, rather than working in a big office doing accounts. I'd done that in my earlier working life, but now I had the luxury of working in an environment that suited me. And my dining-room-come-study was exactly what suited me. I could have Classic FM playing in the background and get as many cups of coffee as I wanted, all day long. When I'd worked in offices, I'd been frowned at for putting the kettle on umpteen times a day.

The Thompsons seemed such a lovely young couple and were a breath of fresh air after Doreen and Elsie, who had lived on either side of me before. They'd been perfectly nice, but were both elderly and only seemed to talk about their ailments and their continual hospital appointments. I'd taken each of them to every one, taking my laptop with me and doing the less detailed work in the waiting area. I always parked myself next to the hot drinks machine, even though it didn't produce great coffee, at least it had a faint resemblance to a drink from a ground bean. When I moved, they both said they didn't know how they'd cope without me, so I found some leaflets about the volunteer patient transport scheme and put one through each of their doors. I didn't like to think of them unable to get to appointments, but at the same time I wanted to make a new start.

I did rather miss helping them, so I said to the Thompsons that I'd be happy to take Hamish for a walk from time to time, so that he wasn't on his own for too many hours. I said it made sense, given how hard Tyler and Caitlin worked. They were delighted with the idea and soon, from "time to time", turned into every day. It was lovely having someone pleased to see me even if that someone was only a dog. He'd run up and down the hallway, bringing me his soggy ball. His hairs were a bit of a nuisance clinging to my trousers, so I bought myself some of those sticky rollers that lift hairs and lint off your clothes, so I could always have a tidy up when I got home. Our favourite place was Riverside Walk, going into the town and then crossing over the bridge to walk along the canal. I loved looking at the canal boats and often saw familiar faces that I'd say hello to and pass comment on how good or bad the weather was.

The Thompsons must have had to work even longer hours than when I first arrived, because I noticed how they got home later in the evenings now, sometimes so tired they almost seemed to stagger. I was glad to have saved them having to go out again with Hamish.

I'd often thought of getting a dog of my own, but I was always worried it would prevent me doing things. What those things might be, I'd never stopped to really think about. I wouldn't describe myself as antisocial as I had friends and I met up with them every week or so for a cup of coffee or to go to the cinema. I kept in regular touch with my brother too. But I loved solitary things as well, like doing the gardening and most of all, cooking.

It wasn't just being allowed to share their dog, that I'd got the Thompsons to thank for, they let me look after Destiny too. Never having had any children of my own, I was delighted at her little antics and imaginative games. She was six when I first met her and still into teddy bears picnics. She loved the miniature sandwiches and cakes I made for the stuffed guests. We played all sorts of games and she seemed to enjoy my company just as much as I did hers. She didn't seem to mind if her dad and Caitlin were busy and I was asked to look after her all day Saturday and sometimes Sundays too.

But it got more difficult to entertain her as she got older and she didn't want to play board games anymore. It was quite hard to fill all that time and I had to resort to letting her watch some TV. We always went into town for a little shopping trip to New Look for accessories and Superdrug for make-up, but it did get quite expensive if I didn't set a limit for Destiny to stick to. It was a shame Tyler and Caitlin had to work on these visits, but as they said, even at the weekends, people need to look at houses to live in and old people needed looking after. I knew if they had been able to change shifts to spend more time with Destiny, they would have done.

Everyone knows that it's not as much fun cooking for one as it is for a family, so I also had the pleasure of making delicious rich casseroles for them, which they collected after they got home from work. My friend Jenny said I should join the dinner party club that she belonged to as I enjoyed cooking so much, where you took it in turns to have the group round. She said it was a really interesting bunch of people so they had fascinating conversations as well as having different food to try. I said I had too much on, and thought to myself, who needs dinner parties, when you've got grateful diners next door. And they were so easy to cook for. When I had my brother staying with me a few years ago, I remember he complained if something was too spicy, or if I had put too much salt in. He told me he wasn't a fussy eater, but from the comments he kept making, I found that hard to believe.

Jenny also stayed with me for a week more recently when she'd twisted her ankle and I suppose by then maybe my cooking had improved. Certainly I didn't put salt into most things. She was good at saying what had worked well and what hadn't, so I knew I could trust her judgement. And she definitely liked most of what I made.

Destiny of course, didn't eat the same things that her dad and Caitlin did. She was too young to wait for them to get home for dinner when I first looked after her, so I became a dab hand at chicken nuggets and potato waffles. I did insist she have some peas with them at least, to try and add some nutrition. She likes pasta best now, which is also nice and easy to cook, or pizza. We had quite a bit of fun making our own pizzas one weekend, when we rolled the dough out and got flour everywhere. We'd gone to the supermarket and got the toppings specially and it was really tasty. Sometimes at the weekend, they'd ask me to babysit for Destiny and so I said of course I would, it was just as easy to watch their TV as it was mine. It wasn't as if I'd have a long walk home afterwards. But they did get home rather late and I found myself nodding off on the sofa. I then struggled to get to sleep when I got myself into bed, as I'd woken up again going out into the cold night air. So we altered the arrangement and Destiny slept in my spare room when they knew it would be after midnight.

Destiny liked the novelty of it at first, but then grew bored with the lack of technology. She asked me how I managed to survive without an Xbox or a PlayStation in the house. I often thought my looking after Destiny, gave me a taste of what it would have been like to have a daughter. This sometimes saddened me that I'd missed out on something special, but then she started getting argumentative and it didn't seem so lovely after all. Her being moody and withdrawn I could understand, but she had started to say some rather hurtful things. I was sure it was just things she'd heard in the playground and bless her it was really her hormones talking. But I did stop thinking of motherhood as being all rewarding and fulfilling, and replaced it with a mixed bag of emotions that were certainly not always positive.

My business was now taking off very well and although I hadn't gone looking for new customers, I found I kept being recommended. If it carried on at this rate, it would mean I'd have to either take on someone to help me or turn people away. I rather liked being in that position because it had been hard work getting established in the first place, so it was gratifying that I'd made a success of it. I had to be more organised now with other aspects of life. Hamish got a walk into town, but had to skip the canal now and I'd tie him up outside Waitrose whilst I went in to shop for the evening meal. I usually went every day as ingredients for three, or if it was the right weekend, four people, meant it could get heavy to carry otherwise. I was determined not to use the car for short journeys and prided myself I was doing my bit to save the planet. I needed it at night and for trips to see my friends further away, so I felt I was entitled to its convenience then. I had to use it to visit Jenny as she lived out in a village and the buses had stopped running there regularly. I ought to visit her more often really as she was quite lonely with no one living that close to her. She wasn't as lucky as I was. She didn't have a Thompson family to be part of.

Before I got so busy with work, I'd spent quite a while looking through my large collection of recipe books or looking online for ideas. I liked to offer up something new, but it had to be capable of staying warm in the oven and not drying out as Tyler and Caitlin were quite unpredictable about when they got home. We had the agreement that the first of them to come home, would pop round and collect the dish of the day from me. I always collected the dirty casserole dish when I went in to take Hamish out the following day.

It was the evening that I made coq au vin, topped with cheesy scones, that it happened. Caitlin had taken it from me, smiled and went into her own house. It wasn't until after she'd gone that I realised I hadn't told them I couldn't take Hamish out next Friday, because I was going with Jenny to London. I walked up their path and was about to ring the doorbell, when I heard them talking, quite clearly as the windows were wide open. My finger was just about to press the button, when I heard Tyler's voice.

'What revolting muck has she brought us today, eh?'

'She said it was chicken and I don't know, something cheesy on top, I wasn't really listening.' Caitlin said.

'Stick it in the bin.' Tyler replied.

'Not all of it,' Caitlin said, 'pick out the chicken for Hamish.'

'Is she going to babysit Destiny on Saturday? Alex's party should be wicked.'

'Didn't ask. But, of course she will, she's got nothing else to do.'

'True.' Tyler replied,

'She keeps saying she's so lucky to be part of our family, so she can do something to help for a change.' Then Caitlin broke into an impression of me 'Oh Caitlin, you and

Tyler are so dear to me. I so like being able to help, you both work so hard. And Destiny is a little treasure.'

Tyler laughed. 'You got the old bat spot on. How old do you think she is? Seventy?'

'I don't know, maybe.' Caitlin replied.

'Shall I stick some burgers and chips in the air fryer?'

I didn't stay to listen to Caitlin's answer. I went straight home and just sat, staring at the living room wall, shaking. I didn't take Hamish out the next day and turned the radio up when I heard him barking. I felt bad for him, but not so much that I could bear to step inside their house. And how could I possibly manage it on my seventy year old legs? I'm not sure what was the most hurtful, aging me by nearly twenty years, using me as free babysitting or throwing away all that lovely food I'd worked hard for and paid for. Surely they must have liked some of it.

I put a note through their door when they were at work, saying I wasn't well so wouldn't be able to see them or Hamish for a few days. Not until after the weekend at least. That'll stop you going to Alex's party, I thought with a small sense of satisfaction. I said I was sorry to let them down. It's funny how you can put lies down on paper, so much more easily than saying them out loud. I carried on with my bookkeeping and tried to absorb myself in that, but I found I kept bursting into tears without warning.

Then I got a phone call from Jenny. I poured my heart out to her and at first she was sympathetic, until she said she'd tried to tell me a thousand times that they were taking advantage of me, but I hadn't listened. I remembered that yes she had said they seemed to be using me rather a lot to help with Destiny and then she'd said wouldn't it be better for Destiny to see her dad more? If I wasn't so accommodating, perhaps he'd be forced to put his foot down at work and change shifts. But I'd answered that he would surely have tried that and so he must be doing his best. Now it was as clear as day. The pair of them had been doing their best to have a good time without taking their responsibilities seriously either as parents or as dog owners.

Jenny said that my realising what they were really like, was the perfect opportunity to start living a proper life. I told her I missed Hamish most of all and that I'd be cutting my nose to spite my face, if I didn't carry on taking him for walks. She said that was nonsense, I should get my own dog instead. But they're such a tie, I answered, I wouldn't be able to..... And that's when I knew she was right as there wasn't anything I would have to stop doing and for the few times I'd go on holiday, I could put the dog in kennels or get a friend to look after it, just as everyone else does. She said we should go to Appledown Rescue Centre the next day and see what they'd got. Before I knew it, I'd rung them up and a time agreed for Jenny and I to visit. I knew Eaton Bray quite well so I found them easily enough. Which is where I fell in love with Rocky. As their dogs are strays, they couldn't tell me which breed he was but he was definitely a mixture of a few.

Caitlin had knocked on the door after the weekend and it was probably for the best that I hadn't known beforehand that she'd call. She asked if I could look after Destiny on Saturday and that Hamish was missing me, so would I be up to taking him out again? She even had the gall to say they'd missed my home-cooked meals. I hadn't realised I could be good at lying straight to someone's face, but there I was wearing my most sympathetic expression, saying I wish I could help, but it just wasn't possible. I explained my sister was ill, so I'd need to keep going over to look after her. And I was having her dog Rocky too, probably permanently, so I wouldn't be able to take Hamish out again. I even added, Rocky didn't like other dogs or children apparently and that I felt terrible I couldn't help any more with dinners, or Hamish or with Destiny. Caitlin looked at me, as the implications of what'd I'd said dawned on her and she mumbled ok.

Now three months later, I've got nothing but kind feelings towards them. Without them I'd never have adopted my gorgeous Rocky and I wouldn't have gone to Jenny's dinner club. She was right all along. They were such a great bunch of people and the food was amazing. I was so nervous when I hosted for the first time, but it couldn't have gone better. My coq au vin with cheesy scones went down a treat and they even asked for the recipe. As I don't cook family meals anymore, I don't need so much worktop space, so I treated myself to the fancy coffee machine I'd been longing for. Now I can have cappuccino and latte whenever I like and it's easy enough to put away when it's my turn for dinner club. Rocky loves me taking him down the canal and I have struck up some proper friendships now with the regular moorers. I still silently thank the Thompsons for helping me live a richer life. I'm so lucky to have such good neighbours.

Where Did She Go? *(Ruth's Tale)*

The teenager stood before me, wearing a cold expression. I was sitting on a dining chair, too frightened to move but almost as frightened to stay. My back hurt where I'd been shoved down on the chair, banging me into the wooden back with more force than necessary to make me comply. She'd been in the house about an hour now. She wasn't alone. A boy had arrived with her, not a boy really, probably in his early twenties. I'd known there would be more visits, but I'd not expected there would be two together.

I can hear him moving around upstairs now. It sounded as if drawers were being dropped on the floor, but I couldn't work out what else the noises might be. I wanted to pick up the phone and call for help. I could see it on the side table, not ten feet away. But it might as well have been a mile away. She paced in front of me. She'd exhausted looking through the few bits of paper that were lying around.

I looked again at the photos on the wall, trying to draw strength from them. My beautiful daughter, Bella. The first one was her lying in her cot, fast asleep. She had a fuzz of downy hair, pale, not even dark enough to be blonde. Then of her in the garden, maybe two years old. She was wearing the bright pink wellies she'd loved so much and even wore to bed one night. There's a jump to her being about six, sitting on her grandad's knee, cuddling Pebbles the cat. Her hair was long there, golden and slightly wavy, framing her smiling face.

She was such a lovely child. She'd help me whenever I asked her, actually loving washing up and plunging her hands into the bubbly water. There may have been more water out of the sink than in it by the time she'd finished, but nothing got broken. She was so careful. The next photo was when she was ten, on stage in the school production. She'd been so excited to have been chosen to play Wendy in Peter Pan, she'd never stopped repeating her lines around the house and was beside herself when the opening night was a huge success. The final one she was thirteen, not smiling, but not scowling either, just a nod towards being independent by not complying with the request to say cheese.

And then she was gone. And I still couldn't comprehend it. How could it have happened? I came out of my reverie when the teenager spoke again. She pressed her face close to mine. I could see the fine lines around her eyes, blackened with mascara and eyeliner she'd applied heavily. Her hair was short and in black spikes, cut haphazardly.

'Where's the money?' She shouted at me and I recoiled from the noise and from her venom.

'I don't have any.' I said. I wanted to shout too, but I was afraid. I felt a tear roll down my cheek.

'Oh spare me the waterworks.'

'Sorry.' I mumbled. I decided I needed to try and reason with her. 'You don't have to do this.' I said as steadily as I could.

'No? You going to hand over a stash of gold bars instead then?' she screamed at me. 'We need at least a hundred quid. I know you've got stuff worth at least that. And cash.'

'I spent my last bit of cash on paying the milkman this morning.' I said, so softly that it was almost a whisper. I used that trick when Bella was a little girl. When she'd got herself worked up about something and her volume had gone higher and higher into hysterics. I would use calming words, spoken quietly, empathising and showing her I understood until she calmed down enough to listen to reason.

The teenager stomped out of the room, not responding to my tactics. I thought she might check there was milk in the fridge from a dairy rather than a supermarket brand. She wouldn't find either. I long ago gave up eating properly and my clothes hung off me now, but I couldn't bring myself to choose new ones. She came back into the room. I could see she was weighing up whether or not to challenge me on my virtually empty kitchen, but she hadn't found anything to contradict the milkman story, just nothing to support it either. I held my breath, waiting for her next move.

The boy ran down the stairs and came into the room. 'It's all rubbish. Nothing we can sell.'

'Haven't you even found the gold rings and the crucifix?' She asked impatiently. She strode across to me and yanked my hands from my lap, letting them drop when she saw they were bare of any jewellery. I had on a blouse today, with a v-neckline, so she could see I wasn't wearing the necklace either. I didn't tell her I'd dropped it down the sink when I knew I'd lost Bella for good. And my faith in God along with her.

'We're wasting our time. Let's go.' He said. He was jumpy and I could see track marks up both arms. They matched those on the teenager.

'Go where?' She shouted at him. 'We've got to get it to him today. You know we have.'

'All right, don't shout.' He said, retreating from her.

She strode across to me and held her hand up, ready to strike me. 'One last time. We want jewellery or money. Now where is it?' She pressed her face into mine and I could smell her stale breath.

'I spent the last of my money on the milkman and I lost my rings in a burglary.' I met her gaze, knowing she'd remember now that she was the one to have wrenched them off my fingers only a few months ago, despite me begging her not to, not my wedding ring. Her eyes dropped and so did her hand, back to her side.

I wanted to look at baby Bella again. That photograph was by far my favourite. It was the one most likely to help me hold it together. But I couldn't afford to look away from the angry person in front of me. Anyway it wouldn't be for much longer. It wasn't last time, or the time before.

'What about a bank card, you must have one of those?' The boy asked, stepping towards me. He put on a brave swagger, but I could see he was as frightened of her, almost as much as I was.

'Yes, yes, I have,' I answered, grateful I could give them something that would make them leave. 'It's in my bag there. The PIN number is 2254.' I didn't tell them there wasn't more than a couple of pounds in that account, just enough to keep it open. I'd long ago worked out that it was best for me to have nothing, then she couldn't take it from me. So my wages went into a different account, one that paid the rent and bills straight away, leaving me enough for groceries and whatever I wanted to buy. I managed it online, so I didn't have a paper trail in the house. I didn't keep a computer or smartphone here either, the phone was at work and my home phone had to suffice for whatever calls I needed to make. And cash was best kept at work too. Having it too readily available here, would only make the visits more frequent as I'd be rewarding them for their effort in turning up.

'You better not be messing us about,' he said as he took it out, 'else we'll be back.'

I nodded, knowing they would anyway.

'Come on then, let's go.' He said and headed towards the front door.

The teenager hurried after him, but stopped at the doorway and looked back at me.

'Bye Bella,' I said to her, the familiar pain returning to my chest.

The Journey from Paddington *(Janet's Tale)*

It's all because I was reading on my Kindle. I must confess I was rather against the devices when they first came into the shops. I was quick to spout how it would be the death of printed books and they were soulless. That holding a book, a proper book, had a quality that these electronic gadgets simply couldn't replicate. And then my daughter Briony bought me one for my birthday. It was a Paperwhite she said, so you can read it in sunlight in the garden or in the darkness of the bedroom. When I opened it, I must confess my heart sank somewhat. I could tell from the weight of the box that it was something modern and had guessed at a new smartphone. She was all pleased when I took the lid off and she told me she knew I'd love it once I got started on it.

'It'll give you a whole new lease of life,' she said.

There's no denying how much I love my daughter. She was the only child my husband and I were blessed with and I confess we've spoilt her terribly over the years. Our pensions are somewhat depleted after we gave her money for a deposit on her first home. But I sometimes think I'd live in complete poverty if it would make her happy. Since Alan and I retired, she's been even more the focus of our lives. We can't wait to become grandparents, although that might be a while off as there's no boyfriend on the scene. In the meantime, Alan helps her with decorating the little 1970s flat she bought and doing DIY with her. And I've made curtains for the living room and bedrooms.

Being as close a family as we were, I found it hard to fool Briony. I chose instead to pretend I would need help setting up the Kindle, rather than my objection to the thing itself. She seemed perfectly content with my answer and said of course she'd show me. I'd get the hang of it in no time. She said how much easier it was when you were travelling. I didn't like to say I didn't really travel anywhere anymore, I just nodded and said how handy it would be on a plane, when you had to watch the weight limit of your luggage. She busied herself on her notepad and set me up an Amazon account.

It took me a while to get used to it, but I became familiar fairly soon with the main tasks I was using it for. I chose an Agatha Christie to get me started as I had enjoyed them when I was a lot younger, but not gone back to them recently. And I discovered how much I liked reading in bed. Alan didn't particularly enjoy reading, so when we got into bed, he didn't want me sitting there for ages with the lights on, keeping him awake. Now of course I could sit there with my book lighting itself up. Briony had bought me one of those special covers for it, which meant it turned itself on and off when you opened it up. As I slept on the right hand side of the bed, the cover screened the small amount of light pollution that emitted from the screen, so Alan could go to sleep lying next to me. I was good at keeping still whilst I read, so it worked a treat.

Sometimes when I sat up reading, I looked across at my sleeping husband and wondered where the years had gone. What had happened to us? I could still remember the days that we would both be eager to get to bed and that certainly wasn't to read. It was hard to think back to the last time we had sex. It wasn't from any row or dislike on either part, we'd just sort of drifted from it. I didn't really have the urges I once did and I suppose I assumed Alan was the same. I thought about asking him, but it seemed a difficult conversation to start. Perhaps I'd pluck up the courage sometime soon.

I had to go down to Bristol to visit my sister, so I thought taking the Kindle would be perfect. Briony was pleased when I told her how much I liked reading in bed now. Next time I spoke to her, I'd tell her how useful it was on the train. I had to cross London from where we are in the suburbs and then it was straight down from Paddington in just under two hours. Alan usually comes with me as they get on very well, but he'd got a hospital appointment and given how precious they are, he couldn't afford to turn it down. I'd offered to go with him, but he said it was just the routine follow up and he felt fine, there wouldn't be anything amiss, he was sure. So I agreed, knowing he didn't like me fussing over him. I suggested we move the date for going to Bristol, but it was my sister's birthday and she'd got this thing about always wanting to celebrate on the day itself, so I really had to go then. We agreed we'd schedule in another visit soon, for both of us and for Briony to come too.

The train was busy, but I managed to sit down by the window, in a cluster of four, around a table. The seat immediately to my left was occupied by a young woman, who was desperately trying to contain a lively dog on her lap. Opposite me was a middle-aged woman who'd closed her eyes and was resting her head against the edge of the window frame. She'd also got a Kindle, with the smart black cover, just like mine, which sat on the table just in front of her. Next to her sat a man reading the free Metro newspaper, the remains of a cup of coffee in its takeaway cup was in front of him on the table. I rather liked watching people and so I didn't open my Kindle to start with, just set it down ready for me.

The dog was rather a nuisance and the woman's attempts to distract it and offer treats, were all in vain. It just wolfed them down and clambered over her, licking her face, whilst she mildly protested.

The dog, I think it was one of those designer things that doesn't shed fur, looked cute but was either still young or the owner hadn't trained it very well. It launched itself out of her arms and climbed on the table, knocking the coffee over the newspaper and somehow pushing the two Kindles onto the floor. I bent down and picked them up and was confident I was giving the right one back when I sat them both on the table.

'I'm so sorry' the woman said, then in a ridiculous voice, she spoke to the dog. 'Buttons, say sorry to the man and the old lady.' She pretended to make its mouth move and said 'Sossy' in what she must have assumed was a comical voice for a dog. I wasn't amused by her attempts to apologise as I was rather reeling from the old lady description. After all I was only sixty eight, no age at all these days. I was too polite to say anything, but just smiled. She got more treats out of her bag and handed them over.

I couldn't look their way after that, so I picked up my Kindle and went to delve back into the Evil Under the Sun. It took a few lines before I realised it was an entirely different book. The words were, well, they were utter filth. I read on several pages and it was all in the same vein. I thought I must have pressed on some key that had taken me somewhere I hadn't intended. There were a whole list of free and ninety-nine pence books I'd downloaded, that I knew nothing about, so I assumed I'd made my way on to one of these. I remembered how Briony had shown me how to get back to the home screen and my library. When I'd gone there, Evil under the Sun was still not showing and when I looked at the pictures of what the covers of the books were, well I was shocked.

It wasn't just the pictures, the titles were really rather rude or racy at the very least. Of course I realised now that this wasn't my Kindle at all. I looked across at its true owner in surprise, but she had her eyes closed still. I was relieved really. I don't know quite what my expression betrayed. I closed it up and was about to swap them, when I stopped. I had been truly taken by surprise when I'd seen those images, but the one with the young couple, him stripped to the waist and her in some lacy underwear was really very compelling. I found myself opening the Kindle up again. I scrolled through the library and saw more that were equally pleasing. It took me another moment to realise that my long lost urges, were making a return.

I had just come to the decision that I would swap them back now before its owner woke up, when I looked across and realised I'd left it too late. She was looking out the window, so hadn't realised what had happened yet. I decided to wait in case she nodded off again. I sat there, holding her Kindle, very keen to look at it again, but at the same time, desperate not to get caught doing so. In the end my curiosity got the better of me. I selected one of the titles and started reading. I was starting to think there couldn't be anything else that would shock me, when it happened again. The words were, well I've never read them in such sentences before and descriptions so vivid of intimate acts. I really wished I was at home with Alan at this very moment. I read on, completely unable to stop myself.

All too quickly the train pulled into Bristol Temple Meads. The woman and her dog, as well as the man with his damp newspaper had already left at earlier stations and I hadn't noticed. The woman opposite was standing up, also preparing to leave now. She opened the Kindle and realised straight away that she was holding mine.

'You've got the wrong one, I believe.' She said.

I looked at her, feeling like a rabbit caught in some headlights. I didn't want to hand it over. I didn't want to give up the rejuvenation it had brought about. I'd started planning taking Alan out to dinner and ordering lots of wine, remembering that had always got him more in the mood. And those picture, those words had definitely had the desired effect on me.

'No I haven't' I said. 'This one's just right.'

She smiled a wicked, conspiratorial smile. 'Okay, but I think the one in my hand is newer than the one in your hand.'

'That's okay.' I answered.

'Well no problem then. I can download it all again from the cloud.' She said as she took my device and we both stepped onto the platform.

I scurried away from her and sat down in the coffee shop to catch my breath. And then I laughed at my audacity. This wasn't me, I didn't do things like this. But Briony had been right all along. Having a Kindle was giving me a whole new lease of life.

The Birthday Surprise *(Justin's Tale)*

If there's one word I'd use to describe my Jessica, it's predictable. It annoyed me sometimes, such as when we went out for a meal and she'd always choose the same thing. And it wasn't even to have anything decent, it was fish for Heaven's sake. She'd always say she couldn't cook it at home because I complained it made the flat stink. Well it does, but she could have it round at her mum's.

Jessica and her mum were very alike and it depressed me sometimes what Jessica would turn into when she was older. But I consoled myself I could always trade her in before it got too bad, if it came to that. Not that I was exactly James Bond material myself, but good looks don't matter so much for a bloke. We can carry a bit of extra weight and even have a few wrinkles. Makes us look distinguished. But women can look haggard when they're all crinkly.

Jessica was a few years younger than me, so hopefully she'd last out all right. In fact it was a significant year for me, I was going to be forty. And that explained why Jessica seemed to be spending so much time with my mate Adam. They were planning a surprise. I was hoping for a party in the room out the back of The George. The beer was pretty good there and you could hire the room out and they'd organise a disco and a buffet. Jessica's good with money, better than me really, so she's bound to have enough put away for it. She's taken some out of the joint savings already, which will be for the deposit not doubt.

I have to say I am relieved at what she's up to, because I had been worried for a while that she'd found out about Shelly. She's the receptionist at the garage where my poor car has had to go back and forth to be fixed. But it is a Merc and I love driving round in her, so I didn't have a choice but to pay out to get her repaired. Which has meant I've spent quite a while waiting around there. I could tell Shelly was bored with her job, so I cracked a few jokes and made her smile. I've always had a knack with women. Shelly hadn't long broken up with her boyfriend, so she was ready to have a bit of attention paid to her. I didn't mind doing that. And when she let me in after hours, my Merc was there ready to oblige us with some privacy and a comfy back seat. Seen a bit of action, that seat has. Not recently with Jessica, but there's no need when we've got a double bed at home. Not that she's much in the mood, even with me trying out my best lines on her, she'd just say she's heard them all before and make excuses about early starts to get to the office.

I told Jessica I don't know why she bothered going all the way to London, if she hated commuting that much, but she says can't do her job working from home, so she has to get up early. Because there's rent needing to be paid and there's finance on the car. I leave all that paperwork up to her, I can't be doing with reading all that small print. All I care about is having somewhere nice to live and something nice to drive. And a decent phone of course, money for eating out and drinking with the lads and some decent clothes. I'm a simple guy really, with simple tastes.

Jessica hasn't always worked there, but she got made redundant from the local one, and as she hadn't been there very long, there wasn't much of a pay-out. So she found this other job, but it's a bit of a trek. Apparently she's quite specialised, so there wasn't anything else nearby. But she gets back in time to get us a bit of dinner, so it's not that bad.

Shelly started getting a bit needy, wanting more from the relationship than I did. I did let her down gently though and gave her the old line that it was me not her and I just wasn't ready to leave Jessica. Actually I started with that line, but when she still kept pestering me, I told her Jessica was really ill and needed me more. She gave up then. I've seen in the past how women have got a loyalty code, to not nick someone's bloke if they really need them.

Jessica said her girlfriends were coming over on Friday night and would I go out for the evening. I thought that was a bit rich and toyed with the idea of seeing what Shelly was up to, but I couldn't be doing with all her clinging again. So I said I'd see what my brother was up to, he was usually good for a trip down the pub. Luckily he was free, so I left them all to it. Even though we stayed out quite late, the women were still in the flat when I got back and it looked as if Jessica had been crying. I went to bed and watched a bit of the footie before I went to sleep. I asked her the next day if they'd upset her, but she just said no, they hadn't, so I let it go. I didn't really want her going on about them. Sometimes I got the feeling they didn't like me, which is quite unusual as women usually love me.

I'd asked my brother if he'd got an invite to my fortieth, but he said he hadn't. It was only a month away and I thought Jessica ought to be getting a move on, otherwise some of them wouldn't be able to come. It's tricky though, because if it was supposed to be a surprise, I could hardly tell her I knew. I thought I might ask at The George and they confirmed they had got a booking on the Saturday my birthday fell on, but wouldn't tell me any more than that. Data protection they'd said, which is such a load of nonsense, but they wouldn't budge. I was due to see my mate Adam again soon, so I'd ask him.

When I did meet up with him, it was very odd. He's never been good at keeping secrets, so he was probably trying to keep his promise to Jessica and hold up to my questioning him. All I could get out of him was that Jessica was definitely planning a surprise. Well, knowing that and the fact that the George had a booking, well it was all coming together, so I decided to enjoy the anticipation. I hoped she hadn't gone stupid and said no presents. I'd gone to a couple of parties and they'd said that on the invite. I find that notion quite ridiculous frankly, after all, that's half the fun. I wondered how many pint glasses I'd get with forty on them and thought well you can never have too many beer glasses.

As we got closer to the day, Jessica got even more distant than usual. She said she thought she was coming down with something, but whatever it was, it was taking a blooming long time. Never mind, I thought, it wasn't long now. Surely on my birthday we'd have a bit of fun.

On the day itself, she gave me a card and said that the rest would come later. Before I could get any more out of her, she said she had to dash. Well, that was a turn up for the books. I was at a bit of a loss really, thinking we'd do something together, go out for lunch if nothing else. After all, you didn't always have all that much to eat at a buffet. Not if some greedy pig has got in front of you and some of my mates could definitely be described as that. I decided to have myself a big fry- up. I quite liked cooking that, it was the clearing up that I hated, but as it was my birthday I could leave it for Jessica for later. I watched some rugby after that and had a nap on the sofa before I woke up excited about the party.

It was strange that Jessica hadn't returned by six o'clock. She usually took ages to get ready and I hoped she wasn't going to make us late. I had a long shower and thought it served her right that I'd used up all the hot water. Getting dressed I'd started to get a bit annoyed. I'd left two text messages and three voicemails by now. Then it occurred to me it was all part of the surprise. She'd know I'd head over to The George sooner or later on my birthday. Of course, that was it. I'd walk in there as if to have a pint and one of the bar staff would tell me to go into the back room on some pretext, then they'd all shout out at me. I thought I'd better practice in the mirror, to look surprised. I gave it a go, but even I didn't think I looked genuine. Still, it'd probably be fairly dark, so it would be okay.

I didn't need to take the car because it wasn't far. When I got there, I could hear noise coming from the back room and I smiled to myself. I went over to the bar and said hello to Phil. He seemed a bit distracted and handed me an envelope whilst he poured my pint. I opened it up, thinking Jessica had really gone to town with getting me to the surprise party. I expected it to say a couple of lines, perhaps come into the back room or something like that. Instead, Jessica had typed two whole pages. I sat down and sipped my pint.

At first I thought it was some kind of elaborate joke. But when she said she knew all about Shelly, I knew it wasn't. Despite this, I couldn't help peeking into the back room, still not convinced there wasn't a party waiting for me. There was a party in there, but some old geezer's retirement do, by the look of it. I sat back down and felt my heart sink as I read on. She said that she'd forgiven me for Robyn, but now she'd found out about my latest affair, she'd had enough. She said she'd given notice to our landlord and so I'd only got a fortnight left in the flat. I was pretty gutted at all this. It was a lot to take in. This wasn't how I was supposed to celebrate my fortieth. Losing my girlfriend was one thing, although truth be told I wasn't all that bothered. After all, she'd been quite frosty for a while, now I think about it. But losing the flat, well that was a blow. I'd lived with my Mum before Jessica and I rented this place. I was not looking forward to going back to that.

My mate Adam must have sided with Jessica and that's why he was off with me. He didn't usually judge a bit of extra-curricular activity, although ever since his wife had it off with the bloke at the supermarket, I suppose he had changed his tune a bit. At the time I'd joked, to try and cheer him up, that it was like that old cliché, the housewife doing it with the milkman, since that's where she got their milk from, that supermarket, but he hadn't found that funny. They got divorced after that.

Just as everything was sinking in, she hit me where it really hurt. Apparently the Merc was never in my name. It was bought on PCP, whatever that means, and Jessica had paid the balloon payment and so now she owns it. And by the time I read this, she'll have driven it away.

I just sat there. How could this be happening? This wasn't my predictable Jessica at all. And then, as I thought about my beautiful Merc, I suffered the ultimate embarrassment. Just when Phil was looking across at me, I felt a tear run down my face.

Other People's Children *(Anna's Tale)*

Friends often asked us why we did it. We told them that yes, it was difficult, but then there would be some small success that made it all worthwhile. It's twenty years now that Pete and I have been foster carers and at the beginning, although we didn't have any experience, the kids were straightforward. We were given short placements whilst their families were sorted out, either parents taking the children back, or other relatives stepping in.

Our first real challenge was Todd. He had been with three foster families before he came to us. I don't think the social worker thought we were ready for someone like him, but she was desperate. We said yes, it would be no trouble, but soon realised how wrong we were.

Todd was worldly way beyond his nine years. His mother had died when he was a baby and his father was an alcoholic. If he'd stayed drunk, they could have taken Todd away properly and given him a new home. As it was, his Dad managed to get his act together just enough to convince a judge at every case hearing, that he was a changed man. He usually had a new woman in tow, just to add to the picture of providing a good home. The women didn't stick around for long and those that did, also ill-treated Todd. His Dad kept saying it was Todd's behaviour that drove him to the bottle and everyone accepted that must be true. Including Todd.

Even though it was only a short time we'd been doing this we realised that if you tell a child the same thing often enough, they will come to believe it. Especially negative things. Their fragile self-esteem and confidence were easy to crush. And when it was gone, anger and attitude filled the gap. What Todd realised, was that he had very little control in his life, but the one thing no one could make him do, was talk. When he arrived at our doorstep, he'd already been silent for five months.

He'd only been with us a few days, when he was asked to do his art homework in the dining room. But instead of the still life drawing he'd been asked to do, his picture was of big black clouds, with a devil like creature looking down. At first we didn't know what to say. And then I noticed the pencils. My beautiful set of fifty colours, normally organised like the rainbow in their special tin, was now of one hundred short ones piled in a heap. Todd had a look in his eye that invited an argument.

'Todd,' I said, as levelly as I could, 'The picture is technically very good, but you'll still need to do the task the school has set you.' I gave him a fresh piece of paper.

He nudged the pile of pencils and they cascaded over the table, spilling out onto the floor. Pete saved the day then. He got out the pencil sharpener and set it down on the table.

'You know it was wrong to destroy the pencils,' he said 'but we'll make the best of it. I'll saw off the sharp ends and you can sharpen the others. Off you go.' He walked out and gently led me away too. Through the gap at the edge of the door, we could see him sitting there, his arms folded.

'What are we going to do if he just ignores us?' I'd asked Pete.

'I'll hide the TV remote.' He whispered.

We carried on watching Todd and then to our surprise, he started sharpening. And he carried on until he'd finished. Pete went back in. 'Thank you for doing that Todd,' he said. Todd, as expected, made no reply, but picked up an orange one and started on the homework he'd been set. By the time the picture was finished, it did resemble the fruit and I thought he should know how good it was.

'You've got real talent you know Todd,' I said, trying not to sound patronising or talk down to him. Sometimes it was just so difficult to know what the right words were. Here it was easy because I genuinely thought he'd made a good job of it for a nine-year-old. Clearly Todd didn't know how to handle any kind of praise and he stared at me whilst he tore his picture into tiny pieces. Before I left the room I managed to say, 'you'll have to do that again. School still needs it handing in.' I got as far as my bedroom before I started crying. Pete tried to comfort me and say I'd done the right thing, but it didn't feel like it. It felt like failure.

After four months with us, we'd made some progress. He still refused to talk, but he'd stopped reacting badly whenever he was complimented and so I'd gently persisted. He was behaving better at school too.

My brother's family came over one Sunday lunchtime and we all sat at the table. The serving bowls were passed round and everyone seemed happy, the food disappearing fast. At first, I didn't realise something momentous had just happened, until it was repeated, and louder.

Todd was stretching his arm as far as he could, but still couldn't quite reach the bowl of Pete's legendary roast potatoes.

First quietly and then with some vigour, Todd said 'Tatoes.'

I could have cried and had to force myself not to rush across and hug him. As usual, it was Pete who did the right thing.

'Tatoes please,' Pete said holding the bowl close to Todd but just far enough away that he still couldn't get to them. And Todd repeated both words straight back.

We've had many more kids in our care, but nothing touched us like that early triumph in our career. Todd comes to visit us in the holidays, when he's back from uni. He's loving his art course.

Homemaker *(Nico's Tale)*

I never understood why some were so chirpy when they woke up in the morning, being all cheerful and letting the world know it was a new day. I liked to come to gradually myself and didn't take kindly to any kind of squawking waking me up. Except today. Today I was in fine spirits and keen to go over to see my darling Leila. My mates couldn't see why I liked her so much. You could describe her as strong, not suffering fools gladly and she certainly spoke her mind. That's the bit they didn't like, as she was rather fond of telling them some home truths. I didn't care she called me lazy and a waste of space. She was right and she was right for me, as I couldn't get her out of my head.

She'd told me she was old-fashioned in some ways and she wanted someone to be a good provider, someone to help make her home nice. Where we could bring up some little ones. I liked that idea, of me being a dad. I must be growing up at last.

I'd got the idea yesterday when I was passing a pet grooming parlour. It was such a lovely day, they'd got a few of them outside being brushed. Fur was flying everywhere, you wouldn't believe the amount that came out of them. It surprised me how people liked pets as much as they did. They were a lot of work after all and expensive. And the idea of keeping birds in cages, really upset me. It just wasn't natural.

I decided I'd go and visit Leila first thing, see what sort of mood she was in. Then I could take the surprise round to her. Her place was easy to find and I waited patiently, but it was clear she had gone out. I debated what to do next. Should I go and make the collection and hope she was here when I came back, or wait first to see her? I hung around for a bit and then had a little nap.

When I woke up there was still no sign of her and I decided I'd see if any of my friends were out and about. I looked in the usual haunts but didn't see any of them. I ate some peanuts that were put out for whoever wanted some and then went home. Feeling at a bit of a loose end, I thought about having another nap but realised I really would be the lazy good for nothing she already thought me to be.

I decided I'd go back to the pet parlour and collect it straight away. When I landed on the fence which kept the animals enclosed, I looked down and saw that they were all inside today. But the spoils from yesterday were still there, caught in the bushes and tumbling around on the grass. I flew down and pecked at various clumps of fur to find the best bits. Some were hard to grasp hold of, but I was very pleased when I found some large bundles of super-soft white fur. Leila couldn't fail to be impressed. What chick doesn't like fur I thought.

It wasn't too far to fly over to her nest and my heart soared when I saw her sitting there. She turned and looked at me when I approached. I'm sure she was impressed when she saw what I had in my beak and when I'd dropped it into the nest she definitely looked pleased. I told her that I'd got it specially for her. That I wanted to be the homemaker she wanted me to be, a good provider. She hopped around, feeling the texture and agreeing it was indeed extremely soft and would make the nest very cosy indeed.

I thought I'd wait for her to spread it out and snuggle into it, before I asked if I could stay the night. My hopes were definitely up now as I saw how much she liked it.

Then suddenly everything changed. She screeched at me, what did I think I was playing at, bringing this into her beautiful home. I kept asking her what on earth did she mean? Didn't she like it? Why didn't she like it?

No, she answered, she most certainly did not like it. She hadn't been able to place what it was at first but then it came to her. This wasn't from a poodle, it was cat. She batted me away with her wing and tried to peck me as I didn't immediately move, too stunned at how quickly everything had changed, to be able to think straight. I apologised and told her I hadn't realised, I'd only seen them grooming dogs. I offered to get her some more, but that was it, I'd blown it. I offered to pick it all up and take it away but she was having none of it. I left feeling very dejected. Blasted cats, the bane of my life whenever I wasn't flying around and now spoiling my chances with Leila.

I told my friends afterwards and they couldn't stop laughing. They were all relieved I wasn't with her any more. Then I saw this chick on the next branch looking across. I hopped over and asked her if she'd like some dog fur to line her nest. She was delighted at the thought and said what a nice touch that would make to her home. I puffed up my feathers and asked her where she lived. With any luck, I might get invited to stay the night.

The Eighty Pound Rule *(Brittany's Tale)*

Matt had very fixed ideas on what was the right thing to do, it's just his ideas didn't always match mine. This wouldn't be an issue if I hadn't agreed to his suggestion. But I had and it would have been wrong to have gone behind his back. I reasoned, this wasn't the same. No, not the same at all.

He'd come up with his famous "eighty pound rule" about a year after we'd moved into the flat together. It was after we'd bought several big things to make it more homely, a nice rug for the hallway, a small table and chairs for the dining area in the kitchen and the TV for our bedroom. But afterwards, there were sales on, in which each item we'd paid full price for, was heavily reduced, sometimes down to half the price. Matt had been really upset and said we had wasted our money and people who wasted things didn't deserve to have anything nice. It occurred to me that his family had tried a bit too hard to instil responsible values in him. I managed to have a better perspective on things and argued that we got a bargain sometimes, but not always. I also reminded him that the things we'd bought, we had saved up for, so we weren't wasting money by getting them on credit.

But he wasn't himself for days after that. Until that is, he came up with "the rule". He said in future, whenever we needed to buy something costing more than eighty pounds, we should wait until the sales were on. I asked what would happen if there weren't sales for a particular item, but he said every shop had one sooner or later. What about if the washing machine breaks down, would that count? Surely we wouldn't have to wait for a sale then. We'd need to get on with replacing it, if it couldn't be fixed. He conceded that for an essential article like that, it could just be replaced straight away. Anything else, we should wait. And because he'd looked so sad for those few days, but his little face lit up when he was explaining his great new idea, I said yes. I promised him I would not buy anything non-essential over eighty pounds, unless it was on sale.

I'd been very good. For seven months. Seven very long months when I'd seen things that I would love to have owned, but didn't meet this new rule, had been and gone from shop windows, never reappearing in any sale.

Now, I'd got my heart set on a new pair of leather boots. My current ones barely left my feet from when the sandals went away for autumn and out came the boots instead. And they were lovely and comfy, not worn down at the heel or the leather toes too scuffed. But they were a bit on the scruffy side. I tried every polish I could think of to smarten them up, but they were creased from constant use and nothing could hide that. Despite my desire for a new pair, the current state did not mean that they passed the exception test of an essential broken article. I would have to wait for a sale. I even rang the shop and asked them when the next one might be, but they said they never got told by head office until a few days before. Maybe after Christmas they might. That was no good. I couldn't wait three months. I just couldn't. I had mentioned to Matt that I'd like to replace them, but once he knew how much I thought that would cost, he said, sure, when they were on offer.

I waited until after he'd finished work on Friday and when I heard his key in the door I pressed the play button again. He walked in and gave me a kiss as always.

'Hiya' he said, 'what are you watching then?'

'That second Jumanji film,' I replied, 'I'll put the kettle on in a minute.'

'Cheers' he flopped into the armchair and kicked off his trainers.

When the adverts came on, I left the room and made him a cup of tea.

'Walk This Way have got a sale on' he said, 'I just saw the advert.'

'Have they?' I asked, as innocently as I could.

'You could get some new boots. We could go tomorrow if you like, we're not doing anything.'

'Yes, sure,' I answered as calmly as I could, secretly rejoicing inside. After a few minutes he said he was going to change and went off to the bedroom.

As we walked along the High Street the next day, I started telling him about the funny thing Sylvia had said at the office. He always said she was the weirdest person we knew and loved hearing about her latest exploits. This time it was the tale of her trying to dye her hair red. So he was laughing when we went into the shop. I went straight over to the ankle boots and soon found what I wanted. I asked the shop assistant for the other shoe in size six and she disappeared out the back. I continued to entertain Matt with another story I'd been keeping back, for just this moment. Bless him, when he was smiling at me I felt a bit guilty. But when I had the boots on, that completely vanished.

'How do they feel?' he asked.

'Great.' I replied, 'and so much smarter than my others.'

'How much will that be then, in the sale?' he asked

'Oh, it doesn't say. It's just got ninety-nine pounds, ninety-nine pence here,' I said pointing at the box.

'Excuse me,' he said to the assistant, 'are these not in the sale?'

She looked at him blankly. 'We're not having a sale. Maybe after Christmas'

'But it said on the TV, up to half price.' He looked upset as he tried to explain and somehow convince the assistant he was right and she was wrong.

'It's funny, a woman rang up asking if we were. But we're definitely not. Sorry.' She walked away to another customer looking for his second shoe.

I stood looking at the beautiful, shiny black leather boots and let out a loud sigh. 'I better not have them,' I said and very slowly took them off, taking my time putting them in the box, stopping short of actually stroking them.

Matt had a pained expression and I knew he was arguing with himself.

'Right you scruff bags' I said, picking up my old ones. 'It's you and me together a bit longer.'

'Oh why don't you treat yourself to the new ones?' He said at last.

'They are more than eighty pounds.' I said. But not wanting to talk him out of it, I quickly added, 'oh well, if you're sure,' and walked as fast as was decently possible, over to the till.

All the way home he kept saying he couldn't understand it. The advert had definitely been for Walk this Way and it was everything up to half price. I just murmured how odd. I could have pointed out that I'd been watching a recording of the Jumanji sequel, which had originally been shown in January, when the shop did indeed have their after-Christmas sale. But then he might have realised I tricked him and I wouldn't want that. After all, I wouldn't have needed to if he hadn't come up with the silly rule in the first place.

The Extra Plate *(Sarah's Tale)*

She opened the kitchen cupboard with a sense of trepidation. If she got it wrong, it would provoke a reaction that she just didn't want to cope with this evening. She glanced at the table and at her daughter sitting there, staring back. Looking at her pretty face, no-one would guess what she could unleash. Sarah decided she would have to risk it and took three plates out, putting one in her usual place and drew in her breath before putting one in front of Gemma. The third she set down in the place next to her. Their eyes met and Sarah thought that she had judged it correctly.

'He's not coming.' Gemma said matter-of-factly.

'There's still time. Dinner won't be ready for another ten minutes.'

Gemma gave her the look she had come to expect. That of her superior knowledge over George. Although no one could know George in the way she did. He'd begun as her friend and then after a few months, Gemma had started referring to him as her boyfriend. It went from George being mentioned in casual conversation, to Gemma talking about him incessantly.

Sarah had to ask before each meal, if he was coming too and was told off for being unwelcoming if she hadn't got him a plate. Sarah wasn't at all convinced that the relationship was healthy and when she tried to talk to her daughter about seeing other friends, she was rewarded with the silent treatment for several hours.

Sarah even arranged for her old colleague to come over for a cup of tea after school, knowing she'd bring her daughter Holly with her. Her hopes of Gemma being a good hostess were dashed as she watched her grab a slice of cake and disappear upstairs, making it perfectly plain no one was welcome to follow her. Sarah smiled and apologised that Gemma didn't seem very sociable today, but Holly made a less kindly comment and it was obvious there would be no point in repeating the experiment.

She tried to talk to Gemma later and said she was disappointed at how rude she was.

'I didn't want Holly over.' She replied, 'I wanted to be on my own.'

Then finally she'd given the news Sarah had been waiting for, that Gemma and George had split up.'

Sarah took the empty plate away when she put the bowl of spaghetti down in the middle of the table. Gemma scooped out a large portion for herself and tucked in. Sarah wasn't at all sure what her next move should be. In the end she decided to take the plunge.

'Are you all right about breaking up with George?' She asked.

'Yes.' Gemma replied, stabbing a meatball with her fork.

'Maybe it's for the best. You can spend time with your other friends.' She suggested. 'What about having Libby round?'

'No I don't like Libby.' She answered, tomato sauce dribbling down her chin.

'Why ever not?' Sarah asked, disappointed as she was the sweetest little thing you could wish to meet. She couldn't fathom what had gone wrong between the two of them.

'She didn't like George.' Gemma replied.

'Well, that won't matter now.' Sarah replied.

Gemma gave her another of her well-practiced looks of despair. 'When we get back together it will.'

Sarah was taken by surprise as she hadn't expected there to be a reunion. 'Oh. I hadn't realised you might do that. So he's just a friend again now is he?'

'Yes. But he's not coming today, because of his allergies.' Gemma had previously given her the longest list of allergies imaginable, which included cabbage, broccoli, peas, beans and horses.

Sarah wanted to know which of them he thought would be present in their house today, as they didn't have any pets and none of the foods were on the menu. They were all foods Gemma didn't like anyway, so that hadn't been hard to accommodate.

Sarah got up and put her plate in the dishwasher, still wondering how she could encourage Gemma to mix with more friends. That was when Gemma surprised her again.

'Actually, I don't think I will have George back.' She announced.

'Why not? Anyway you don't need to decide now.'

'Well he's not real.' Gemma said staring at her, as if to see if Sarah had thought all along that he was.

'I know,' Sarah said, 'but he was real to you.'

She went to walk out of the kitchen when Gemma's scream, halted her in her tracks.

'What?' Sarah asked.

'You were about to walk into Tatti' She said crossly.

'Tatti?'

Gemma let out a sigh. 'Yes Mother. Tatiana. My unicorn.'

Off My Trolley *(Patricia's Tale)*

If I hadn't run out of milk, I'd have stayed inside that day. But I can't stand black coffee and I needed the caffeine to get me going. I needed something stronger than that really, especially as my ankles were giving me gyp, but it was far too early. Shaun would have massaged them for me. I missed those little things, that he used to do.

I thought maybe I should go back to Dr. Pratley, but then I remembered the way he looked at me, when he'd said 'of course your ankles hurt. It's to be expected with that touch of arthritis you've got, but mainly having to carry around all fifteen stone of you. For your height Mrs Somersby, that's simply too much.'

'Any chance I might still grow a bit doc?' I'd asked, hoping for at least a smile from him. But no, he'd probably heard that one before.

Instead he'd asked, 'Would you like me to refer you to a dietician?'

'No thank you,' I said, rather offended, 'I know what isn't good for me.'

He looked as if he wanted to add that I shouldn't eat it then, but he let it pass. He said I should use this painkilling gel and I did give it a try, but it was ever so messy and when I put my socks on, they stuck to me. Then he said I should exercise to lose some weight, which was very easy for the old prat to say, but how could I do that when my ankles hurt?

It was drizzling outside and I decided I'd get the bus. If I took my shopping trolley with me I could stock up a bit while I was in town. And I could have my cup of coffee in Morrison's café before I did my shopping. Better still, I could have one of their nice cooked breakfasts. And if I chose mushrooms and beans, that would be two of my five a day. Shaun would like me to try and be healthy. He'd be cross if he could see me now. I used to be quite skinny and I even like to think I was rather attractive once, but that seems a long time ago now.

I thought I'd better give the gel another try. I rubbed it in as best I could and walked around with bare sticky legs whilst I got my bits and pieces together. It was a good job no one could see through my net curtains as I did look a sight in my jumper, knickers and no trousers as I didn't want the bottoms of them to get sticky too.

I put my hood up as I walked towards the stop and I hadn't been there long before the bus turned up. They were pretty reliable and I didn't mind using them as long as they were going where I needed them to. If I wanted to get to the doctors it was all right at their original place in Leighton Road as there was a stop close by. It was when they sent me to their other place up Grovebury Road that was tricky. Ridgeway Court it was called, but it went over two buildings, one round the corner to the other. The first time they said I had to go there was like being in Alice in Wonderland.

'That appointment is at Ridgeway Court.' The receptionist had said.

'Where's that?' I'd asked.

'Grovebury Road.'

'Oh, Grovebury Road Surgery. Yes I've spotted that when my son's taken me to the Grove Lock pub. They do lovely meals there.'

'No,' she replied sharply, clearly not someone who would appreciate good food with a nice view of the canal thrown in. 'It's not Grovebury Road Surgery. It's Leighton Road Surgery. Next door.'

'So where does Ridgeway Court come into it?' I asked.

'It's in Grovebury Road' She said as if talking to a child. I decided to get a taxi that time and let the driver work out where I was supposed to be. They've merged the two surgeries now, probably because no one could find where they were supposed to be going.

When I got on the bus, I walked to the front row of seats where I could have my trolley with me and sat beside the window. There wasn't much to see because it was so misted with condensation. We'd just pulled away when a young girl came and sat next to me. I suppose she wasn't very young really, maybe 17 or 18. She tucked some headphones into her ears and I could hear a tinny repetitive beat begin. I suffered this for about five minutes before I'd had enough. I nudged her gently and mouthed to her, could she turn it down please. She sighed and took one of the headphones out and I could now hear the words being sung.

'What did you say?' She asked, not giving me any confidence that she actually cared what my answer was.

'I said you'll go deaf if you have it that loud.'

She put the headphone back in and looked away.

When I arrived, I got up and pulled my trolley after me. I mumbled sorry as one of the wheels ran over the girl's foot, but really I was only sorry it wasn't yet full of heavy shopping.

I felt better after my late breakfast and was happy choosing some food for the rest of the week, so I didn't notice my ankles too much for a while. They did start to hurt badly again when I was queuing at the bus stop to come home. The others there were mostly pensioners with trolleys, and somebody with one of those push along walking things that doubles up as a seat. The bus was already crowded when I got on and we were all packed together, with this wheeled seat thing in the way. I was lucky to be able to sit down, although a woman who was a bit older than me, gave me a dirty look. I wanted to tell her I was in pain and so I deserved the seat just as much as someone elderly, but I just looked away.

A mum with toddlers on each arm got on at the next stop and made a fuss about not having enough room, so there was more shuffling about. I moved my trolley out of the way and then after more jostling I was face to face with a cute little baby. She couldn't be more than six months old, her chubby little hand clasping a plastic ring with different coloured balls bouncing around inside. I smiled at her and I was rewarded with a lovely smile back. It quite cheered me up, until I realised her expression was linked to some nappy related activity and I was glad to get away from the smell when it was my stop.

I rested for a few minutes before unpacking the trolley, but I took the bananas off the top and put them straight in the fruit-bowl in the middle of the table. Shaun always called it that, but since neither of us ate any fruit except bananas, I sometimes referred to it as the banana bowl. It annoyed him when I said that and so if I was cross with him over something, I'd say it on purpose. I'd love him to be sitting across the table now, making me cross.

I looked at the bananas and thought they seemed a bit smaller than the ones I usually got and greener too. I suppose they must have looked different in the lights at Morrisons. I put my hand in the trolley and pulled out a carton of eggs. I didn't realise I'd got more of them as there was definitely still some still in the cupboard.

It was pulling out a tin of cat food that really upset me. Tigs hadn't been seen for three years now. He'd gone out in the morning and just never came back. He was a stray when I found him, so whenever I was sad that he'd gone, I liked to think that was his true nature, a wandering soul and he was with a new family now.

I felt a sudden sense of dread at the possibility I'd got early dementia. It was the first sign wasn't it, getting confused with periods of time? When I was in the supermarket, had I really thought Tigs was still living with me? Even if I had, why did I buy this tin of Whiskas? He always had those pouches that didn't smell so bad, but squirted the gravy over you, when you tore the top off.

I put my hand in the trolley again and pulled out several more items and put them on the table in front of me. Muesli! Why on earth would I have bought that? It tastes like cardboard, even when they have fancy names and freeze-dried bits in it. There were some tins of beans and soup, which looked different to my normal choices and then some washing-up liquid. I looked at the trolley and felt rather frightened. What on earth had I been thinking? And where was my pack of doughnuts? I distinctly remembered picking those up. They had six different iced toppings, so much nicer than the ones filled with jam. My fright had changed into being annoyed at the loss of my favourite treat.

It was therefore a huge relief when I realised that the trolley wasn't mine. The buckle that held the outside pocket closed, should be missing, but there it was, shining straight at me.

Once I started laughing, I couldn't stop. I really had worried myself. I bit into one my bananas before I realised it wasn't mine either. I rooted around in the trolley to see if there was any label or other way to identify the owner and sure enough, Mrs I Wilkins had written her name and number on the inside. Good job she had, as there wasn't anything in mine to link it to me. I carefully dialled the number, and it was several rings before she picked up. Whilst I was waiting, I imagined myself in some kind of film and pictured myself negotiating a handover. You've got something belonging to me and I want it back. She'd haggle and we'd meet somewhere neutral and release the trolleys only when the other one was in touching distance. However, when she answered, I knew I had to be sensible.

'Is that Mrs Wilkins?' I started with.

'Yes.' A brusque woman answered.

'I've got your shopping trolley.'

'Thank goodness.' She said 'You didn't put your name in yours. Didn't your mother tell you to label all your belongings?'

'Only when I was at school.' I wouldn't have a word said against my mother. She was one of the few people in my life that loved me, just as I was.

'Where are you?' She asked.

I gave her my address and it turned out we were pretty close by. She said she'd come to me. I filled up the kettle and switched it on, thinking I would offer her a cup of tea as she'd made the effort.

She stood on my doorstep, and I recognised her from the bus journey. She was the one who'd given me a dirty look.

'Come on in, do you want to have a cup of tea?' I asked, hoping she didn't recognise me.

From the way she said yes, having a sit down would be nice, I gathered she had.

I'd put her shopping back already, but I did have to apologise about the banana. I offered her one of mine, but she said no thanks, they were too ripe for her liking.

'Don't you think they've got a funny texture though,' I said, 'when they're still green.'

'Yes,' she said. 'The texture of a banana, not all slimy, which is how they go when they're bright yellow.'

I didn't know what to say to that. It wasn't like me to be lost for words. I busied myself pouring out the drinks and sat down at the table with her.

'They're ever so useful, these trolleys, aren't they.' I ventured.

'Yes, I suppose so,' she replied.

I thought this was a perfect opportunity to put the record straight. 'I have a lot of problem with my ankles.' I felt better having said that.

'You're a bit young for that aren't you?' She said, looking straight at me as if trying to guess my age.

'Yes, a bit. I'm only 65. But it's arthritis all the same. Very painful.'

She nodded and I felt she was warming to me. That was until she said, 'I expect the doctor's told you to lose weight.'

I was about to say it was none of her business and she could forget the tea and clear off. But before I had the chance, she carried on.

'I was a lot like you ten years ago. Except my problem was my bad back and being about four stone more than I should be. I was thirteen stone instead of about nine.'

'Oh. You don't look like you were ever that heavy.'

'It was after Frank died. I took to comfort eating.'

'I'm sorry to hear that. Were you together long?' I asked.

'Not as long as some. Only 30 years. He just dropped down dead, out of the blue with a heart attack.' After a minute she said, 'Are you married?'

'No. Shaun used to live with me. But I've lost him now.'

'When did he die?' She asked.

'Oh he's not dead,' I replied. 'I lost him when he went back to his wife. Don't know why though, she's a miserable old cow and devotes her life to making him miserable. But he couldn't stay away from her for too long. He felt responsible for her because she's not right in the head.'

'I don't approve of affairs.' She sniffed.

'Nor do I really. It just sort of happened. You know, two lonely people making each other feel needed.'

'And what would his poor wife have felt?'

'Miserable, I know. But she's miserable when he's there too, so why should all three of us be unhappy. That's what I think.'

'Won't he ever leave her?'

'No.'

'Well you might as well find someone else then.' She said as if it was as easy as choosing a new coat.

'No one's going to look at me when I'm this big, are they?'

'Of course they will. Overweight doesn't mean unattractive.'

'I don't feel attractive and if I don't, then I can't expect anyone else to see it in me.'

'Well lose some weight then. And your ankles won't hurt so much.'

'I don't know how to. I've tried every diet there is going.'

'Including the donut diet. I wonder why it hasn't worked. You do know it's not true, the calories don't fall down the hole in the middle.' She said.

I was about to give her a sharp reply but to my surprise, she started laughing.

'What's so funny?' I asked.

'You are. You're just like I was. Feeling sorry for myself.'

'Well how did you manage to change then?' I asked, curious as to how she'd made such a difference to herself.

'Aqua aerobics. Down at the Leisure Centre. Lots of jumping up and down in the water, didn't hurt my back like it did on a floor and puffed me out no end. What with planning my meals better with what I should and shouldn't eat, before I knew it, the pounds were falling off.'

'Bet you still missed Frank' I said, thinking I'd still miss Shaun even if I was a size 10. Not that it was that likely.

'Course I did. But after a while there was Derek. And then Philip, and Jack, then Roger, no, no Roger came after Mark.'

'Blimey, you were the merry widow.'

'I was. And Frank would have been proud of me and given his blessing. Whatever makes you happy, that's what he'd have said. Wouldn't Shaun want that for you?'

'I suppose so, yes. It's been two years since he went. He won't be back now, not this time. It's been too long.'

'Well then. Time to stop moping and start sorting yourself out.'

'You don't beat around the bush, do you.'

I said to her.

'When you get to my age, you can't waste a single minute.' She looked at her watch and gulped down her tea. 'And I must go, I'm expecting Jeff soon.'

After she'd gone I thought about what she said. She was spot on. I had been feeling sorry for myself. Right, I thought and I picked up my phone to search for some details. Let's see when this aqua nonsense is on. I suddenly wanted a Jeff for myself. And then maybe an Alan, and a Stuart and ...

The Things we do for Love *(Steve's Tale)*

I generally considered that I was happy with a quiet life, which involved doing as little as possible. Some might say lazy and I couldn't really disagree. I'd coasted through life, from one job to another, doing just enough to get by. I didn't have any regrets about the places I worked, I wasn't treated very well and they didn't get the best out of me, so I figured we were quits. But I should have tried harder for Alice's sake. Her mother and I were a mistake from the beginning. We couldn't keep our hands off each other, but it turned out that was the only thing we had in common. She was sensible, apart from her decision to spend some time with me, and I really was not. And despite being careful, she got pregnant. So a few months after I'd skulked off, Alice was born.

She's the only person in the world I have ever completely loved. My mum, well, we got on, but we banged heads as she wanted a better life for me than I was willing to work for. No girlfriend had ever inspired me to get my act together and settle down, yet this squealy little baby had grabbed my heart with her tiny fist and squeezed tight.

I did improve a bit after she was born. I managed to stay in one job for eight months. That was really quite an achievement for me. Her mum, Jodie was surprisingly tolerant of my irregular maintenance and habit of showing up on her doorstep asking to see my princess. She was of the opinion that Alice should really know me and be able to see for herself who I was. I sometimes think her attitude was to get Alice to decide that I wasn't good enough for her and give me the elbow, saving both of them further aggravation. Well if it was Jodie's plan, it backfired because whenever I messed up with dates or times for seeing Alice, she forgave me and always seemed excited to see me. We did have fun together. I swear she's got my sense of humour and Jodie good-naturedly complains when we gang up on her.

Alice is eight now and she's supposed to be staying with me over half term. She's been over at weekends plenty of times, but this will be the longest. She keeps texting me about how she can't wait and how many sleeps it is until I pick her up. But then I'd got the sack, again, for being late. That was usually the reason and this time the agency refused to find me anything else. I hadn't expected that. I'd always been offered something, even if it was just a day or two before the next assignment started. I knew from the way they spoke to me, that I'd crossed the line this time.

I thought, well, it won't really matter, I'd get some universal credit and just go a bit short for a while. Then they tell me I'm sanctioned, because I was sacked. I tried to argue it was only agency work, which could have ended at any time, but they weren't having any of it. No money for two weeks and then I could apply for hardship payments, which would be less than the normal benefit. The adviser at the jobcentre virtually said it would still be more than I deserved. I wanted to punch the guy, but knew that wouldn't get me my money any quicker, just a trip down the nick.

When I told Jodie what was going on, I never expected she'd say I couldn't have Alice to stay with me if I hadn't got a proper income. Alice wasn't a spoilt child wanting taking out every day and ice creams or hot chocolate in fancy coffee shops. She was a good girl and knew not to ask for much when she spent time with me. But at the moment, I hadn't even enough money to feed her for the week, let alone treats. I'd even gone to the foodbank. They were kind, but the assortment of tinned foods they showed me as an example of the donations they received was underwhelming, to say the least. We wouldn't go hungry but she deserved better than that.

I'd heard of loan sharks, and I knew enough that if I borrowed the money, I'd be in serious danger if I didn't pay it back. And that was the problem. I didn't just have a short-term cash-flow trouble, I was always like this. Even when I got another job, I knew myself well enough that I'd lose it before long. So that wasn't an option. I tried some payday lenders, but their rules had got tighter and I couldn't even borrow from one of them. Even when they wanted to charge me two-thousand percent interest. I wondered how much lower I could sink. Little did I know I was not at the bottom yet.

That's when I met her. The little old lady that looked like a sweet grandmother that knitted and drank tea all day. It was Joe next door, that put me on to her. I'd been telling him what a mess I was in and he said he knew of some work going. But it was a bit, well he wouldn't say directly what, just that the money would be good for the right person. Someone reliable. My mind was doing overtime wondering what I would be doing. I guessed it must be something illegal, I just wasn't sure quite how bad it would be.

My Mum had always said I had an overactive imagination and maybe she was right. It was certainly going all over the place now. I hadn't even met the old lady at this point, Joe had just said it was ready money for someone willing to do as they were told and keep quiet about it. I wondered how far I'd be willing to go. And then I worried that by the time I'd been told what it was about, it would probably be too late to back out. I'd know too much and be a liability. I didn't like the idea of my successor being told to get rid of me. Alice needed a dad, even one as useless as me. She knew I loved her and I tried to convince myself that this was worth more than Barbie dolls and trips to the zoo. On my darker days I found it hard to convince myself.

But if I got caught doing whatever it was she wanted, what would that do to Alice? A dad in prison was worse than no dad at all, surely. Then I thought about my empty cupboards. I toyed with asking Jodie for some money, after all she got child benefit and benefits all year round to top up her part-time job, but I knew that was a non-starter too. She'd say if I didn't have enough for such basics, I couldn't look after her properly. And what sort of week would we have together if it rained all day? I wouldn't be able to even take her bowling.

So with a heavy heart I walked to the address Joe gave me, following the map on my phone, half hoping I would get lost. I'd walked up a track to a bungalow, sitting on the edge of some overgrown land. There was a gate and I had to press the buzzer to get in. And then I met her. The sweet old lady with her little dogs bounding round her.

'Hi, I'm Steve.' I ventured at last, as she stood eyeing me up.'Joe, my neighbour said you were looking for someone to do some work for you.' I almost laughed at the ridiculous ideas I'd had. Fancy thinking someone would finish me off. I'd have to make sure I didn't tell anyone what I'd been thinking, otherwise they might try and lock me up. Alice didn't need a dad in the loony bin any more than in prison.

'Stephen,' she said, 'come in, come in,' and she led me through to the sitting room. Before she opened the door, she looked at me and said, 'do you like dogs?'

I didn't actually. I usually hated the way they bounced up at you, digging their claws into your legs and wanting to lick you. But since she had a couple of, well I don't know what they were, it seemed rude to admit it. 'Yes, of course,' I said, with as much conviction as I could manage. I must have been convincing, because she stood there, staring hard. She turned her head slightly and looked at me. I even wondered if she was having some kind of funny turn. Then she finally spoke again.

'What you're about to see, must remain confidential.' She smiled at me, but not in a friendly way. My previous fears all came back. There was something about her. Something I couldn't put my finger on, but troubling nevertheless.

'Do you promise to keep this between us Stephen?'

'Yes, absolutely,' I answered, summoning up a smile.

'Because I'll know it's you that's squealed.' She met my smile, but this time I could see it didn't reach her eyes. 'Everyone else is family, you see. But I know Joe has good judgement, that's why I'm willing to take the risk.'

'I'm the soul of discretion, ask anyone.' I replied, although I'd never had anything to be discreet about, so it was really an empty offer. It was the best I could come up with. I was so tempted to turn around and run out the house.

Surely I didn't know enough yet to be a threat? But I still needed the money. I knew I had to try and convince her I was trustworthy. 'Joe's known me for years.'

'Well then,' let's go inside, she opened the door and we went in.

I couldn't at first quite comprehend what I was looking at. She offered me a seat, but there were no seats without dogs on them. Wherever you looked there were more dogs. Every size and shape imaginable. And the smell, I wanted to retch but managed to do some short deep breaths to keep the nausea at bay.

She sat herself down in the armchair, where a medium one and a little one jumped out of the way, just in time. 'I'm glad you like dogs Stephen, because as you can see, I've got one or two.'

'Yes. Aren't they lovely.' I managed from I don't know where. I was still struggling with the smell and a large black one seemed to be taking an unhealthy interest in my leg. I rubbed its ears and this seemed to distract him from his original purpose.

'Archie seems to like you. I often think he's the best judge of people.' She said, seeming satisfied with my performance as a first-rate dog lover.

'What work was it that you wanted doing?' I asked, thinking I couldn't bear it in this stuffy room for much longer.

'It's just for a few days, until Jimmy comes out of hospital.'

I worried what had happened to Jimmy, but didn't think it wise to ask for details. 'Oh yes?' I said as casually as I could.

'Yes. His appendix burst. Well almost. They got it out in time, but only just. He's going to be out of action for a little while longer.'

'Is Jimmy your husband?' I asked, willing her to get to the point. My imagination was starting to warm up again.

'No, my eldest boy.'

At that moment the door to the kitchen opened and a short, overweight man appeared. He looked in his mid-forties and although he was fat, he had a threatening look about him. I got the impression you wouldn't want to get on the wrong side of him.

'Ah Frank, this is Stephen. He comes recommended.'

Frank nodded, picked up his phone and disappeared back into the kitchen.

'Frank can't deal with it all on his own. Needs to share the workload with someone until Jimmy's back.'

'What workload would that be exactly?' I felt it was a reasonable question now. I'd been more than patient. Whatever it was this strange family was into, I needed to know and get used to the idea. I had a feeling Jimmy was just as unpleasant as Frank and even minus an appendix, probably capable of doing me some serious damage between them if I didn't do what their mum wanted.

'It's each one, twice a day.' She said, as if that explained everything.

'Pardon?' I managed.

'Each dog. Needs taking for a walk. Twice a day.' She said slowly, as if I was foreign or something.

'You want someone to walk the dogs?' I must have looked confused.

'Yes dear. But you remember I said it had to be confidential?'

I nodded.

'Because that damn RSPCA have told me I've got too many and if I don't get rid of some they'll take some away.'

'What?'

'I know.' She said, with such a sad expression. 'So when the Gestapo come, my boys take them out for a little trip. You don't think I've got too many do you?'

The black one renewed its interest in my leg and I hastily stood up, pretending to take a liking in a little beige and white thing.

'No. Of course not.' The thing growled at me, and I laughed and backed away, desperate not to step on any others.

'You might as well start now then.' She said and handed me three leads. 'You can't take too many at once, otherwise you look suspicious. And you can't do the same route again until two or three days have passed. I know we're all right up this lane, but they need a proper walk every one of them, so you're going to have to pass some houses.'

'Right.' I said, holding on to the leads, not quite believing what I was agreeing to. So here I was, three unruly hounds trying to pull me over as I walked along the canal. All the while, thinking of Alice and how it was worth it so that we could spend the week together.

And then the big one stopped. My heart sank as I reached into my pocket for the small plastic bag. I pictured the old lady as she'd looked straight at me before I left. That uneasy feeling returning. It wasn't anything illegal and I felt some relief. But it would be the worst job I'd ever had. I also knew if I messed up in any way, Jimmy and Frank would have no trouble showing their displeasure. The dogs had to stay a secret. She'd pressed the bags into my hand before I'd realised what they were. Her final words to me as I left the oppressive little house, 'make sure you don't leave any evidence behind.'

As I crouched down, I vowed that when I was lucky enough to get a proper job, I'd never, ever be late for work again.

Bachelor Boy *(Ted's Tale)*

I'd done quite a bit of research about the Greek islands and found several that seemed worth a visit. I dressed carefully, as I always did when I went to the kennels, in my dark blue jumper, which Gina had always said brought out the colour in my eyes. She also used to say dark colours suited me because of my mop of black curly hair, but that had long faded to grey and I had to be satisfied with the old eyes providing a bit of colour. I toyed with the idea of a suit or blazer but thought that would make me look stuffy. The jumper was one of those designer brands, which my son favours, with a small unidentified animal embroidered on. I wondered if that's what made these sorts of things expensive, that someone had to come up with a logo that made no connection to the product but would make it worthy of a few extra pounds.

I looked at myself in the mirror. I missed not having all that hair. Not only was it no longer black, but it refused to grow on my forehead or the very top of my head. What was Mother Nature thinking of? Why would my head need to get cold when I got older? And why was it growing out of my ears instead? I had enough trouble with my ears and didn't need everything muffling any further. I plucked them out when they got long enough, but that didn't half sting. Women didn't have to put up with that. Gina would always have the last word when I made any observation that the fair sex had it easier than we did. She'd start with childbirth and listing everything else that the reproductive system threw at them every month until you were deemed too old to cook a baby anymore.

'Don't go complaining if all you've got is hairy ears to worry about,' she said when I was feeling sorry for myself once. I'd been plucking the longest of my eyebrows too. Two inches one of them was. What on earth was the point of it growing that long? Perhaps if I'd left it alone it would have grown far enough to cover the bald patch on my head. But somehow the mad professor look didn't appeal to me.

'No, that's not all. I have to pee in the middle of the night' Was what I'd replied to Gina. 'Something down there's getting larger.' She'd kissed me then and said it really didn't need to, she'd not got anything to complain about. Again when I'd questioned Mother Nature, why not make the outside bits get bigger, after all, that's what most men longed for, not for the bit on the inside to swell up and press on your bladder at two o'clock in the morning.

I miss kissing Gina. And so many other things, but kissing especially. And her smile. And her laugh. I took a deep breath and tried to think of something else.

'Come on Bailey,' I called to my cocker spaniel and he obediently ran over to me, tail wagging. Poor thing, he thinks we're going for a walk. I got him into the back of the car and drove the few miles to the boarding kennels I'd used before. I was looking forward to seeing Sally again. I pulled into the small car park and Bailey jumped down, sniffing the gravel all around us. I pulled him to the front door, and it wasn't long before Sally answered. She looked as lovely as ever and I felt something stir, that didn't normally trouble me very much these days.

'Hello Ted, Bailey.' She smiled and made a fuss of the dog. 'Come on in.' She led us through to the back of the house and out to where the pets were kept. It was a small place, so they only ever had five dogs at a time, which suited Bailey. I'd tried other places in the past, but they were too noisy.

'So where are you off to this time?' Sally asked. Still smiling, but now I noticed, not as brightly as she normally did.

'Greek island.' I answered, 'Kos'

'Lovely. You'll have nice weather there this time of year.'

'Yes.'

'Bailey is going to have a whale of a time here, aren't you boy.' She rubbed him all round his ears, just how he liked. He looked up at her adoringly. I knew he'd be well looked after here, even if he wouldn't be quite as happy as if he was at home, but it couldn't be helped. I was bothered by how Sally was acting. She seemed upset but trying to put on a brave face.

'Is everything all right?' I asked.

'Of course, yes, fine, all fine.' She answered quickly, too quickly.

I gave her one of my quizzical looks and waited for her to tell me what the matter was. After a while she said. 'All right. I'm not supposed to say anything, but the Pevensys have told me they're selling up, moving away.'

'That's a shame. But you'll find another job soon enough, lovely girl like you.'

She laughed. 'Not quite a girl.'

'Well younger than me,' I replied.

'It's having to find somewhere to live as well as a job, that's the trouble. I live here you see.'

'I didn't know that.' But I should have realised, of course someone needed to be here all the time. I don't know why I said what I did without thinking, but before I knew it I was offering her my spare room. When she looked at me suspiciously, that I might have designs on her, I added, 'because it would be nice to have a bit of extra income from a lodger. Not too much, but you know, help me with the bills.'

Her face changed and she said it was a great idea and she'd think it over. She'd let me know when I got back from Greece. I nearly asked what she meant but remembered in time that I was supposed to be going abroad. I really couldn't confess now that I wasn't going anywhere more exotic than Northampton General Hospital. And that was only for a bit of day surgery, but I knew I wouldn't be able to walk Bailey properly for a few days, so that was why I needed him to be looked after. I could hear Gina's voice telling me I was a vain old man, trying to impress a younger woman. I replied back to her that at seventy-three there was plenty of life in me yet. But she was right, I was a bit vain.

I said goodbye to Bailey and drove away, worrying less about the operation and hoping Sally would say yes. I wondered how old she was, but shook my head as if trying to get rid of a stupid idea. Not old enough for you my boy, I thought.

Sally had been with me for three months, when my neighbour chatted to me over the back fence, saying her mother was coming to live with her. Would I show her the sights, she asked. I'd never met her mother, but I didn't mind being neighbourly, so I said of course I would, be happy to.

Sally and I had got along famously whilst she's lived here and Bailey had loved the extra fuss and walks he got. I decided she must be about fifty, no older and although I'd have liked nothing more than to sweep her off to my bed, I knew it was just a fantasy. I asked her if she'd ever been married and she'd surprised me by saying she had, four times. She said it was always the same, fun to start with, then the arguments, then the affairs. I didn't enquire if it was them or her that was being unfaithful, but I had an inkling it was her. She seemed to have itchy feet and couldn't settle. I knew I was lucky that there was too much of an age gap for me to have tried my chances, because I couldn't have borne being picked up, just to be put down a short while later.

Then she suddenly announced she's moving on, to go travelling. I thought you had to be a teenager to do that, in your gap year before university, but I just told her that sounded fun. Before I knew it she was off, and it was just Bailey and me again.

I hadn't liked being on my own before Sally had become my lodger and now she was gone it brought back too many bad feelings of when Gina first died. I know everyone says it gets easier and it is true. She's been gone four years now and it isn't quite so sharp, but it still hurts. I hated the pitying looks I got afterwards, whenever I'd said I was a widower, so I soon started just describing myself as single, a carefree bachelor.

I decided I'd better do my neighbourly duty and take this old biddy out next door. I noticed a self-drive van pull up a week ago and a bed and few bits of furniture being moved in. I wasn't really in the mood for playing tour guide, but I'd said yes and I liked to be true to my word.

I rang the doorbell and a short, smart looking woman opened the door.

'Hello, I'm Ted. You must be Naomi's mother?' I said trying not to smile too broadly. This was no old biddy.

'Ted, lovely to meet you. Come on in.' She opened the door wide.

'Thank you.' I followed her into the familiar hallway, the mirror image of my own, but painted in blue. We sat down in the conservatory and drank tea.

That was the first of many cups of tea we shared, drunk in several different places including most of the National Trust coffee shops in the surrounding counties. It was about a year after she'd moved in, that she said she wanted to talk to me. I felt some trepidation, not sure what was on her mind and dreaded that she might want to end our friendship, perhaps she'd had enough of living with her daughter and wanted independence again. I sat down, looking at the clock. There were still several hours until she was due to come over. I picked up Bailey's lead. 'Come on boy. Time for a very long walk.' He was happy to oblige and pulled me along, eager to get out of the front door now I'd made the suggestion.

On the dot of seven, Marjory rang my doorbell. I answered it straight away and told her to come and sit in the living room. I'd made a pot of tea already and poured it out as soon as she sat down.

'Now that's the kind of service I could get used to,' she said and helped herself to a custard cream, that I knew were her favourites. After she'd finished it, she put her cup down and looked straight at me.

'You're not leaving are you?' I asked, unable to bear the suspense any longer.

'Leaving,' she said, 'no. I like it here very much. Very much indeed.'

I heaved a sigh of relief. 'That's good. You had me worried.'

'Well, you've good reason.' She looked at me sternly.

'Have I?' I felt like a schoolboy again.

'What do I mean to you, Ted?' she asked.

'Mean? Well, I really like you. I've so enjoyed our trips out. It's been nice.'

'Nice'

'Yes. Well very nice.'

'And what do you think of me exactly?' She pressed on.

I didn't think that I should tell her what I truly thought, certainly not tell her the whole truth. I prided myself on being a gentleman. What went on in my head when I thought about the gorgeous Marjory Durell was not for a lady to hear. And that's what she was in my book, a real lady. Someone with a bit of class, but who was down to earth as well. I floundered. 'You're nice. Very nice.' I said eventually.

'They are the very words every woman wants to hear Ted. That they're nice.' She smiled at me, daring me to smile back.

'Not just nice, I did say very nice.' I said. 'And you are.'

'I want to mean more than that to you, because you mean more than that to me.'

I felt strange, I couldn't quite work out what it was exactly, but I was not myself, that's for sure. I had a terrible feeling she was talking about marriage. And that was something I couldn't do.

'Marjory, I don't know what you want from me. But I'm sure I've said before, I married Gina, and I know she's not here anymore, but I can't replace her.'

'No, I wouldn't want you to. I wouldn't replace my Harry, even though his snoring was a blooming nuisance. He was my childhood sweetheart and I think about him every day.'

'I hear Gina's voice, telling me to stop being silly or to make my mind up over something. I can picture her chivvying me along or going about her normal life and I don't want to lose that. I don't want to lose her.'

'I understand completely. You were married for, what did you say, 41 years? And I was for 39. Neither of us can forget that time. But I'm not getting any younger and I want a bit more out of life.'

I stood up, not knowing what to do next. I could see this beautiful friendship disappearing from me and knew how lonely I'd be after it was over. But I could also see Gina giggling over a silly postcard at the seaside or serving up one of her famous Sunday roasts. I'd never felt so torn.

'You don't have to choose, because I'm not saying I want to take Gina's place,' she said, 'but I want more. I need more.'

'I don't know what to say. You know how I felt about her, how I still do. And you about your Harry. How can I have a relationship with you if it's not replacing him?'

'Well, for a start, I hear she was a wonderful cook.'

'Oh yes, she could whip up a feast with half a slice of bread and the leftovers in the bottom of the fridge.'

'There you go.' Marjory replied, 'I burn everything or else it's half raw. Can't seem to meet anywhere in the middle. So if I was to cook for us, I wouldn't be anything like your Gina.'

'No, I suppose not.'

'What about films?' she asked, 'Cinema or watching a DVD?'

'Cinema.' I answered.

'DVDs suit me fine.'

'Beach holiday or sightseeing?'

'Beach.' I answered and we went on like this for another hour. I thought of my own questions and compared myself to Harry. There were plenty of differences between us.

'So the real question Ted, is whether or not you want to have some new adventures with me?' She looked at me hopefully.

'Yes, I do.' I realised how much I did want to spend more time with her, do more things and share a life. I knew she was right. I didn't have to replace Gina. She would want me to be happy. I could hear her telling me that now.

'Well then,' Marjory said, sitting forward so that there was a tiny bit of cleavage showing above her blouse. I could feel my heart pounding.

'Lights on or off?'

The Promise *(Walter's Tale)*

When Walter first sat down on the train, grateful for his seat, he was sure he would fall asleep almost straight away. But now he was nearing the end of his journey, he was still wide awake. He'd not been able to take his eyes off the countryside, especially since leaving Hertfordshire and now being back in his native Bedfordshire. The rolling green hills were the complete opposite to the fields of mud he'd just left in Belgium. He heard the train's whistle as they pulled into the station.

He knew it wasn't just the excitement of returning home, or the beauty of the surroundings that was keeping him awake. He'd have to face Lucy and before he did, he'd have to decide if he was going to keep his promise to her. When he'd made it, he couldn't imagine the quandary he'd end up in, but the past eighteen months had been so alien that his imagination would never have been able to conjure up what he'd been through.

When he stepped onto the platform, he knew he had to stick to his word. He walked quickly, resisting the temptation to fall into the familiar pattern of a march. Passing the houses he'd seen all his life helped calm him and he began to look forward to seeing Lucy again. And of course his father, although he knew he'd be sad to see how much he was suffering, the stroke having robbed him of much of his dignity. Before long he'd crossed over the canal and was walking to the terraced cottage, where he'd grown up. He paused just for a moment before he raised his hand to knock, but before he could do so, the door was flung open.

'Oh Wally, thank God you're home,' Lucy flung her arms round his neck and held him tightly. He managed to prise one hand away.

'Are you going to actually let me get through the door,' he replied his smile as wide as hers and she took a step back to allow him into the room.

'I've got the fire built up, so come and sit down next to it.' She ran her hand over his arm as if convincing herself he was real. 'My little brother, back home.'

'Are you ever going to tire of calling me that?' he asked, 'there's only twenty minutes between us.'

'No, it never gets boring.' She grinned.

'Dad asleep is he?' Wally asked.

'Yes, he usually is for most of the day now. Probably best you wait until he wakes up by himself, before you go in. I'll put the kettle on and make you a proper cup of tea. I bet it doesn't taste the same over there.'

'Just one of the many hardships a soldier must endure. I bet the King never realised how much we would suffer.' He laughed, but without warmth. If the only problem he had, was not drinking out of a china cup, this would be the easiest war in history. Usually by the time he got to drink something hot, he couldn't care less what it came in or that it tasted metallic at best. Again, he started to doubt, that he could keep to his promise.

'So, are you all right? I mean really all right?' Lucy asked, sitting opposite, leaning forward as if she just needed to be near him.

'Not too bad at all. Tired maybe, but that's all.' He managed to smile at her, knowing what he'd said was a lie. He might not be injured on the outside, but he knew he'd seen things in these last few months that had left their mark on his soul. He suspected he'd never be quite the same man again.

'What about you? Not much of a life for you, stuck here looking after Dad all day.'

'I have four little girls here as well in the week, so that Mrs Melton can work at the Post Office. She says it's war work since there are so many letters and parcels back and forth between the soldiers and loved ones at home, as well as the telegrams, it would be unpatriotic not to do it.'

'That sounds a lot for you to have to do, and no break from caring for Dad.'

'I don't mind. They're sweet really, most of the time. That's my war work.' She paused as if choosing her next words carefully. 'Will you tell me now, what it's really like? You know you promised.'

Walter thought back to the day they'd walked to the woods and collected some fallen branches for the fire. They'd stopped and faced each other when Lucy asked, or rather demanded that he make a solemn promise, that whenever he was on leave, he'd bring it to life for her, what his days were really like. She'd argued that they'd always shared everything, and this was no different. Just because women weren't allowed to fight, was no reason not to know what really went on. At the time, he'd agreed with her. Of course he would. But he sat there now, warm and the most comfortable he'd been for such a long time, and he knew he couldn't burden her with the truth. He couldn't bring that horror, into this home.

So he talked about the hours of boredom, sitting around and the card games they played. He told her of the rats they caught and let go on an improvised racetrack and bet their cigarettes on. He made light of the shelling, leaving out the pure terror whenever they had to advance through the gunfire. And left out the sadness at the sight of dead and wounded men.

'It's mostly the noise,' he said, 'yes, that's the worst bit. It's very noisy. And muddy.'

'It's not too bad then?' Lucy asked.

'No, I think you've got it worse looking after the old man and four girls.' He looked down at his boots, not trusting himself to meet her gaze, because then she'd know just how much he was lying.

The Cake Box *(Zoe's Tale)*

I'd forgotten his birthday, again. I was so cross with myself as I kept doing this kind of thing. Only recently I forgot the anniversary of when we had met, and although Andy said it didn't matter, I could tell that it did. He was such a romantic, that's part of what appealed to me, but then I let him down by being so inconsiderate.

I left the house before he woke up, so didn't see him or any kind of expression of anticipation of me saying happy birthday. I sent him a text with some emojis and thought that at least he would be fooled into thinking I'd remembered in advance and been a proper girlfriend to him.

I had a long list of deliveries to make today, and the traffic seemed against me whichever road I turned into. I was getting behind and I hated that pressure. I'd not long had the job and on the whole I liked it, but not when it was days like today. There was no opportunity to nip to a shop, but I kept hoping that would change later. If all else failed I'd take him out for dinner, but then I remembered, his sister was coming over this evening. Of course, that's why he'd arranged for her to visit today, I wish I'd made the connection earlier. Even if Andy didn't judge me too harshly for lack of a present, she definitely would.

As the day wore on, I got more and more behind. Finally I found the front door for the twenty-odd storey office block that I had four parcels for. There were several companies in the building and the ones I wanted were on the top two floors. I dropped the first three off at the right places, but it was the last delivery where I got really lost. I eventually found it but was then in a different stairwell. I tried to retrace my steps but just got more confused trying to find the lift.

I walked through an open plan office and saw a group of employees huddled together, with their backs to me. Someone was making addressing them and I didn't feel I could walk past them easily, so I waited for what I hoped was a very short speech.

'As many of you know, I went to the bakery today and picked up my order, so I'll tell you tomorrow how that went.

Keep your fingers crossed folks.' He said from behind the small crowd where a little cheer came from. 'And we can have cake after we've all sung happy birthday to Simone, but first I do just need to go through the arrangements for next week.'

I decided this was my cue to leave. I hadn't liked what he'd just said anyway, it felt as if it was a dig at my own inadequacy at forgetting a birthday in my own home. My eyes had travelled to a square white box on the desk that was against the wall, behind a display board. Without thinking what I was doing, I grabbed it and started back to the stairs I'd come from. I laughed at my audacity, as it was so out of character. I might be inconsiderate from time to time, but I wasn't usually a criminal. At that moment I didn't care. I just had to hope that they wouldn't trawl through any CCTV that they might have, to track me down.

There was still no opportunity to get to a shop and when I dropped the van back to work and switched to my little Volkswagen, I was too tired to go anywhere else. The cake would have to do along with the promise of a meal out tomorrow. I then realised I could make that more convincing, by actually booking it, so I did that quickly on their website.

When I got home, Andy and his sister were already chatting on the sofa, each with a glass of wine in their hands. I gave Andy a kiss and he told me they'd ordered pizza. I said I'd just get changed and was pretty much finished when the food arrived. I left the cake box in the hall, wanting to make a bit of an entrance with it. Andy had seemed pleased when I told him I'd booked us a table at Chez Maurice, which was his absolute favourite, but so pricy we only went there for special celebrations. I wasn't sure if it was my imagination or if his sister looked slightly less as if she wanted to punch me, once I'd made that announcement. Well I thought, bringing the cake in will raise me up even further in her estimation.

Unusually the pizza was all eaten up quite quickly and I think they under-ordered. This suited me very nicely as I was about to fill that hunger-gap. I retrieved the cake box and handed it straight across to Andy. I realised as soon as he started to lift the lid, that of course, I should have checked to make sure it didn't have anyone's name on it. Well now that thought had occurred to me, at least I could be ready to blame the bakery.

'This is very thoughtful of you Zoe.' Andy said, obviously surprised by the gesture.

'Is it Victoria sponge or fruit?' his sister asked as if one of those would be the wrong choice to have made.

Luckily I was saved from guessing by Andy's exclamation of delight as he held up a small flower arrangement.

I was about to ask what the hell that was, when he answered.

'A cupcake arrangement. How lovely. You know how much I love flowers, you are sweet.' He smiled at me.

'Well you spend so much time in the garden getting it all looking nice, I thought maybe something you could enjoy that you hadn't had to work hard to grow.' I was warming to my theme and about to try and name the ones in his hand, when Andy read what was on the little card inside the box.

'Oh Zoe, oh no. I'm so sorry.' He said sadly.

I didn't know what the problem was. 'What?'

He turned the card round, so that I saw the four words written there. Will You Marry Me?

'I'm sorry, but I can't.'

'Why not?' I asked before realising that not only was this not a birthday cake, but that I'd seemingly asked him a life-changing question. And he was turning me down.

'I'm already married.' He said, before quickly adding, 'but we separated years ago. We just never got round to being divorced and I got to think of myself as single.'

I was stunned. I thought I knew everything important there was to know about Andy, even though we'd only been together just over two years. And then there was the whole proposal thing. I'd not thought about marriage, I'd got to being forty-six perfectly happily, in and out of relationships. But the fact that we couldn't go ahead and get married, seemed to make me realise, that I rather liked the idea.

His sister piped in that he hadn't seen her for years. He hadn't lied to me on purpose.

This was my opportunity to gain more points, I thought. I looked as sad as I could manage without having any time to prepare in front of a mirror. 'As long as you get that divorce sorted out as soon as you can, we won't let it bother us. Then we can start planning our future.' To myself I thought, and I can start writing things down on the calendar. It had turned out unexpectedly well this time, but I didn't fancy my chances the next time I forgot something important. Like my wedding.

Half Full, Half Empty *(Chrissie's Tale)*

Dan and I were so different, our friends often remarked it was a mystery why we got on so well. I don't think there was any mystery at all, but the very fact that we complement each other makes us strong. Dan loved to pick an argument, or a lively debate as he called it, often over something really trivial. Mostly when we're driving behind someone who's going far too slowly for the road conditions. "What are they playing at", was his usual opener, just as he said a few months ago when we were driving to see his sister.

'We're not in a hurry, so what does it matter?' I answered.

'It's annoying, they should get a move on.'

'They might not be sure where they're going, they've slowed down twice when they've approached those turnings.' I said.

'Well they should pull over and let me past then. They shouldn't be holding everyone up.'

'Maybe they don't think they're going all that slowly; if they're older drivers, they might not like going too fast.'

'Then they shouldn't be on the road.'

That was the point I just laughed and turned the radio up, knowing he wasn't going to be shifted from his high horse. When we'd arrived at his sisters, rather early, she said we could pitch in and help lay the table if we liked. I couldn't resist saying to him, out of her earshot, 'pity the car in front wasn't going any slower, otherwise we'd have been able to just swan in and eat dinner.'

He didn't reply but was rather heavy handed laying down the cutlery.

When I was diagnosed, everything changed.

'Look at that. Weaving all over the place. Probably on a mobile phone.' Dan said.

'Probably' I answered,

'Or drunk.'

'Yes.' Was all I could muster up.

He tried a few more goes, picking out a large man kneeling to weed his garden, showing more of his backside than anyone would care to see.

'Look at that, you could park a bike in that.' He said.

I didn't even comment. It didn't matter anymore. Once we arrived home, he made me a cup of tea and put my favourite biscuit in the saucer.

'Come on, Chrissie, where's my voice of reason gone eh? Dan said, the concern etched on his face. He seemed to have aged years in the last few months.

'I don't know Dan. Perhaps the chemo has shrunk that too.'

'But you've got to fight. The Macmillan nurse told us it can make a difference, positive thinking. And when she said that, I thought to myself, well that's all right then. You'd be hard pushed to find anyone more positive than my Chrissie. But you're not being that anymore.'

'I'm sorry,' was all I could manage, before I put the untouched tea down and closed my eyes. The weeks rolled by in a haze.

I don't know what was different about that day. Maybe Dan's words had worked their way far enough into me that I couldn't ignore them. Or perhaps the real Chrissie wasn't going to be suppressed any longer. The ward looked out on to the car park. Dan was sitting on my bed, holding my hand.

'Look at that red Volvo. Parked right over the line.' He said pointing to the far side.

'Perhaps there was a car over his side when he parked, but they're now long gone and he looks the guilty party.'

'More like they can't park straight. Shouldn't have a car like that if you can't manage it.'

'They might have borrowed it to visit someone.'

'Or they might just not...' Dan turned to me, having finally processed what had just happened. 'Oh Chrissie, you're back.' He said and hugged me so tightly I had to gently push him back.

'It's going to be all right now,' he said, smiling.

I didn't have complete confidence that it would be all right, but it wouldn't be for want of me trying.

Perfect Audience *(Dennis's Tale)*

We'd been shopping for some time, successfully ticking off items on Marcia's list and I suggested stopping for a drink. My previous suggestion of staying home and buying things on Amazon, hadn't gone down well, as she reminded me, for the third time, that the baby was due in less than a week. Even paying next day delivery couldn't guarantee she'd have everything when she needed it as the baby might decide to make an early entrance.

'They do lovely cakes at Room No 9,' I said. 'They might even have a gingerbread man for Jordan.' I patted my grandson on his head, but this seemed to upset him and he started crying.

'Dad, we can't take the pushchair in there. I know it's nice, but for today, we need to stay at street level. Look, here's Costa, that will do.'

I wanted to say it wouldn't really and that it was better to support the little independents, but she'd already got the door open and was heading inside. It was full of mums and their young children plus a lone man tapping away on a laptop. I said I'd sort out the coffees and Marcia could sit down. We didn't usually spend much time together, just us and little Jordan, it was usually Paula that did this sort of thing with her. But Paula was nursing a broken leg at home, so I'd been volunteered instead. I chose chocolate muffins for the three of us and brought them over to the table.

'Dad, that's kind, but Jordan won't eat his lunch if he has that now.'

'Sorry,' I said. I felt stupid. Of course it was the wrong time for a child to have cake. 'Perhaps they can wrap it up and we'll take it home with us.' I offered looking towards the counter for napkins. But it was too late, a little hand had reached out and swiped one. He'd taken a large bite from the middle and managed to get half of it down his Thomas the Tank T shirt.

'Jordan! Oh look at the mess he's making.' Marcia said, hurriedly reaching for wet wipes. The removal from his hand of his beloved muffin set Jordan wailing that he wanted his choc-choc back and managed to grab another from the tray. He looked straight at me as if daring me to try and take that off him, before it too got bitten into.

'Let him enjoy it and he can just have a late lunch today, eh? Why not keep the little lad happy.' I said, trying to lighten the mood. 'Here you have the one that's left. Your mum says I've got to watch my waistline. You don't need to worry…' The words died on my lips as I looked at her enormous bump, which surely couldn't just contain one baby. 'When you're eating for two,' I added.

'They don't say that anymore.' She said grumpily and continued to wipe my grandson's face whilst she let him eat the rest of the muffin.

'So what would you normally do on a Wednesday then?' She asked me.

'Well,' I began, 'If the weather's nice, I'll do a bit of gardening. I walk to the newsagent every morning, so I do the crossword when I get back. Your mum goes out to her little groups, but that's not my kind of thing.'

'You were in the drama club for a long time. You used to enjoy that.' She said, 'I'd have thought going for more roles would be perfect now you've got lots of time to learn the lines.'

'I can't bring myself to go back on stage. Not after The Inspector Called'. I said, shuddering at the memory. My biggest role ever, one I was so proud of being selected for when there were three other men auditioning for the same part. But instead of Inspector Goole asking pertinent, incisive questions, I was only able to have him say "You were mean to her too, weren't you?" whenever I couldn't think what I was supposed to say. If I hadn't been too vain to wear my hearing aids, I might have heard Andrea trying to prompt me with the lines from the wings. Paula said everyone in the audience heard her, so surely I could too. I wasn't sure I could ever live it down and made a big thing of how overworked I was at the office, and I hadn't given enough time to learning my lines.

Everyone was very kind and said not to worry. But I did worry, because it hadn't been true. I'd spent weeks learning them, feeling happy that I knew them and was devastated when I couldn't recall them when a hundred pairs of eyes were looking at me. I knew as the curtain closed on the final performance, that I'd never go on stage again. Thinking of it upset me. I wish Marcia hadn't brought it up. She hadn't been able to see the show and Paula had been kind, only saying I got a bit muddled with which scene we were on. The truth was I missed being on stage and it would have been a great way for me to use my new found time since my retirement. But I couldn't risk it. The garden and the crossword didn't leave me feeling humiliated. Bored maybe, but that was something I could live with.

'Disposable knickers.' Marcia suddenly said. 'Mum insisted I try and find some. I need to go to the chemist again, unless you'd run back for me.'

The look on my face answered that for her. 'You stay here with Jordan then, and I'll just pop and get some. If he gets bored put Peppa Pig on your phone or if you can't get a signal, there's a book in the bag there.' She got up and waddled out the door before I had time to object.

For two minutes, Jordan was happy, but as the chocolate muffins had now been demolished his water beaker firmly rejected, he was on the lookout for some new mischief. He started wriggling in his chair, pushing at the straps as if they might give way under a little bit more pressure. I was worried he might hurt himself. I let him out and stood him next to me, realising my mistake as soon as I took my hands away from his waist.

He ran like lightning to the back of the café, and it took me a few seconds to realise he wasn't coming back. I couldn't help thinking, what was wrong with me, why couldn't I do something as simple as keep control of a two-year-old? I raced after him and whisked him back, placing him firmly on my lap. He struggled against my arm and I resisted the urge to release him. I took my phone out of my pocket, but soon realised I couldn't navigate finding the pepperpot pig or whatever she'd call him. So instead, I leant over and picked up his book with a colourful picture of a car. 'Right' I said, 'Let's find out what the little green car is up to today, shall we?' I said cheerfully and read out the lines. Jordan was not entertained and pushed against my restraining arm, not listening to the troubles the car had trying to find somewhere to park. I couldn't really blame him, it was a ridiculous story.

'Hey, Jordan?' I said. 'Would you like me to make up a special story for you? Just for you?'

He eyed me suspiciously, weighing up if this was going to be worth sitting still for. Eventually he nodded.

'Good, now once upon a time there lived a little boy in the big, big forest amongst some very scary animals. One day..'

I continued with the story, doing the appropriate voices as Jordan seemed quietest with least wriggling when I was the booming bear or the squeaky mouse. He even laughed. It was a few minutes into the story, before I realised that Marcia was standing in front of me. 'Are you all right love?' I asked thinking she looked a bit strange.

'Yes,' she said, 'I've never seen Jordan enjoy a story so much. I really haven't. He's loving it.'

I couldn't have been happier at that moment. I'd done something right for a change.

'Hey, you should come and read the story at the end of toddler group. They'd all love you.'

A new audience, one more forgiving than the last if I made a mistake, they would be perfect. Now that was appealing. I began to wonder what sort of voice I should give a very hungry caterpillar.

Taking Notice *(Richard's Tale)*

He was fast asleep until he heard the unmistakable sound of a door closing. He turned his head and listened for Mary's breathing beside him. He heard it, rhythmic and familiar. His heart raced a little as he realised that the sound downstairs could only mean one thing. He lay in the darkness, frantically trying to work out what to do. Would it be better to stay quietly up here and hope the burglar would only be interested in money and their electrical things? The laptop was down there and the tablet. Both their phones went on charge overnight in the kitchen, so they were on the worktop and that's where the fancy camera was, that Mary had bought him for Christmas. Mary's handbag was hanging up in the hall, so there might be a bit of cash and her cards. If that was all they were after, it would be safest for him to remain where he was.

He could help Mary cancel her credit and bank cards, then claim for everything else on the insurance. He couldn't have cared less if it put his premium up next year, the main thing was that Mary would be safe. He felt sick at the prospect that a stranger would hurt her. But now he worried that it might be jewellery the thief was after, and as most people kept that in their bedroom, he might come in here.

Richard may not have known what to do, to stop Mary leaving him as she'd threatened, but he was damned if he was going to stand by and let anything bad happen to her. He couldn't wait while his imagination ran wild with dreadful things being done to his wife. He knew he could not take the risk that they would come into the bedroom and him be helpless. He couldn't think of anything that he could use as a weapon, so it would be better to go downstairs and scare them away. Yes, that was the best plan. He pushed the duvet off him and put his feet in his slippers. The worn patches where his big toes went, were oddly reassuring. He took a step forward and smacked straight into the wall.

'Ow,' he said, loudly. 'What the hell?'
'Whatever's the matter? Mary asked, panic in her voice.
'Ssshhh,' Richard said, 'there's someone downstairs.'

'Well I'm sure there is,' she answered and put the bedside light on. 'We're on the second floor, room twenty-six.' Then noticing Terry holding his nose, asked 'what have you done to yourself?'

He sank down onto the bed, shooting pains flowing through his nose coming at the same rate as him remembering that they were in a hotel in Cheltenham. 'I was woken up by a door slamming and because I was still half asleep I thought we were at home and so it must be a burglar.'

'And we don't have a wall at home that close to your side of the bed.' Mary added.

'Exactly. My nose doesn't half hurt.'

'Here, let me have a look.' She gently prised his hand away. 'There's a bruise coming up already. You need something cold on it. Let me wet a flannel, that will help.' She got up and padded across to the bathroom.

'Ow.' He said again, as the weight of the cloth made it even more painful.

'What were you going to do to this burglar?'

'Scare him off.'

'How were you going to manage that?'

'I was going to stand on the stairs and say I had called the police, so he should make a run for it while he had the chance. I was going to grab the long umbrella and hope it looked like a baseball bat.'

'That's very brave of you.' Mary put her hand on top of his.

'I couldn't risk him coming in here you see. I couldn't risk you getting hurt.'

'Richard!' Mary looked at him, perplexed. 'You'd risk a confrontation with some unknown criminal, for me?'

'Of course I would.' He looked at her, 'Don't you know I would?'

Mary hesitated. 'Actually, no. If one of my friends asked me if I thought you'd be a knight in shining armour rushing to my rescue if I needed it, I'd have probably said no.'

Richard pulled his hand away and stood up.

Mary got back into her side of the bed and pulled the duvet up. After a pause she said, 'well you can't blame me.

How do I know what you would or wouldn't do for me, when you never talk to me?'

'I do. We talked about loads of stuff when we were eating dinner.'

'Yes, we've sorted out a convenient date to try and book the car in for an MOT. We've agreed that the hedges should be trimmed back because they're getting out of hand and that we don't have any milk at home.'

'There you are then.' He put the flannel on the bedside table and gingerly dried his face with a tissue.

'That's not properly talking. You know it isn't. I asked you if you were happy and you wouldn't say a word beyond, why shouldn't you be. Well you know why you shouldn't, because we just argue all the time. I said before we came away, if we didn't sort things out we'd be better off going our separate ways. There's no point staying together for the sake of it.'

'I don't want to split up.'

'And how would I know what you want? You never tell me what's going on in your head and you never do anything to show me. You never get me any flowers. You even got me a voucher for my birthday. Not a proper present, a voucher.'

'It was for your favourite shop.'

'But don't you think I'd have liked you to have chosen something for me, from my favourite shop? Don't you think I'd have liked you to take notice of what I might want? I suppose you've no idea what my size is, so you wouldn't know where to start.' She puffed the pillow out with more vigour than it deserved.

'Size fourteen tops, twelve skirts or trousers. If it's a dress, size fourteen, but only if it has a fitted waist, otherwise it'll make you feel like you're wearing a tent. You have size four and a half feet, so a four is all right if it's Clarkes, but if it's any other brand it'll be too tight. It mustn't be too flat otherwise your arches ache. You get small to medium size tights, because ones that come as small are too small and you have to keep pulling them up. The large ones are all wrinkly.'

'Richard!' She looked at him, confused. 'How do you know all this?'

'Because I do take notice. I do care. I'm just no good at showing it.' He rolled onto his side, facing away.

'What's my favourite colour?'

'Forget me not blue.'

'Favourite pudding?'

'Tiramisu.'

She moved across to his side of the bed and put her arm on his shoulder. 'I'm sorry. I didn't realise.'

'Well now you do.'

'Were you really going to whack a burglar with the umbrella, to save me?'

'Yes.' After a pause he said, 'I'd do anything for you.' He lifted his arm up and gently squeezed her fingers.

'I told you coming away would help us sort things out. And it has. You know you want to protect me from getting hurt, whatever the cost to you and now I know you cared all along. You're just useless at showing it.'

'Yes.'

'All right, well we can build on that. Your nose is going to have a great big bruise in the morning. If you're lucky, I'll kiss it better for you.'

'If you're lucky I might let you.'

Matching Pair *(Wendy's Tale)*

By the age of fifty-six, I'd been let down so many times that, I had accepted it as normal. First Dad leaving when I was a teenager and only making sporadic contact every few years after that. Then my first husband ran off with one of my friends, not my best one, but a friend nevertheless. My second husband simply said he didn't love me anymore and left as well. Mum had been a pillar of strength to everyone in the family and our mantra was better off without them. The 'them' was whoever was upsetting us, or whichever job we didn't get. I found it hard to feel better off without the job I was made redundant from, especially as it meant I had to give up my flat with its cute little balcony overlooking the canal. But somehow I coped with all the trials life sent me, by putting up a barrier. If I didn't let anyone in, then they couldn't upset me.

When I started my new role at Harper and Hughes department store, I embraced it with the same professionalism that I always did. As the head of HR, I had tough decisions to make and they paid me well to make those decisions. I'd never again have to lose my home because of someone else's choices. I'd bought my flat with the help of quite a high mortgage, only really being able to by working every hour of overtime I was ever offered and having negotiated hard during the divorce settlement. No one was going to be in charge of my destiny, but me. If this job didn't work out, I'd find another and keep putting more into my pension funds ready for retirement.

Some weekends, after I'd finished the work I brought home with me, I felt lonely. I could admit that to myself, but no one else. That's when I worried about what I'd do when I retired. I could join clubs and maybe do some voluntary work, but neither option filled me with enthusiasm. I suppose part of me thought I'd spend my new free time being with someone, although who that could possibly be when I never went on any dates, was a mystery. Maybe I thought by then I'd mellow and start dropping my guard. But for now, working was my purpose, and I did actually enjoy it, so for now I didn't have much to complain about.

Harper and Hughes were a trickier company than I'd first thought. They said that everyone was part of one big family and that everyone mattered just as much as the next person, whether that was sitting in the boardroom or restocking shelves. They said this, but they didn't mean it. I knew because they had given very clear instructions to me, to be as efficient as I could, by limiting wages and having a low tolerance to poor behaviour. No one was allowed to freeload and those not pulling their weight were to be got rid of. I didn't mind that this was their ethos, even though it directly contradicted what was said at the interview. I looked at it simply as tasks to be accomplished and ones that I would accomplish well.

The trouble started with Belinda French from Haberdashery. This was an out-dated department that had far too little footfall and was dragging the rest of the store down. I repeatedly suggested to the board that the department should be radically reduced and that the staffing could then go down from four to one. I was very precise in my calculations. Belinda led that team and with the streamlining I suggested, her expertise would no longer be needed. A grade-one shop assistant could measure up the material customers wanted and hand over needles, cotton and whatever else. I'd heard Belinda talk to customers for hours discussing what pleats should go where and how to make sure curtains hung straight.

I ventured as far as saying this level of help was more consultancy than sales and that we were providing a service above and beyond the amount of profit that was produced. It's fine to sell some needlecraft materials by all means, but take customer's instructions instead of advising them for free. There should also be a much smaller range as the top selling materials would fit into a fifth of the space haberdashery currently took up.

I proposed to move Belinda to Cookware in the hope that she would dislike it enough to resign and thus save a large redundancy payment. It was in Cookware that Gloria Goodfellow worked, a problem employee that no one wanted to work alongside. Cookware itself was a very disappointing section, carrying out of date lines that were overpriced and uninspiring. It was also a department I'd suggested reorganising, but the board had been adamant about keeping it the same. A wife of one of the board members, had set it up years ago and visited regularly to give her helpful thoughts. The husband was too spineless to stand up to her. Unfortunately, his majority shares meant no one could stand up to him.

When word got out about haberdashery, I hadn't expected the backlash that came. My normally quiet but efficient assistant Louise, plucked up the courage to ask if it wasn't too late to rethink the department's restructure. I told her it was pretty much all decided and asked why she was concerned. She told me that Belinda's husband had recently died and that she was saying it would be like a second bereavement to lose her beloved department as well. And to have to work with Gloria every day would likely be the death of her too.

Of course I'd known about the husband. Belinda had taken time off and made use of the company's bereavement payment as well as taking some time off sick. It had added up to a tidy sum, so of course it hadn't got past me unnoticed. I told Louise a fresh start would probably be much healthier for her and left the room before she could reply.

I was very fair in all my dealings and made sure everyone got the pay they were entitled to as soon as it was due. If they had medical problems, I invoked the company sickness policy and made reasonable adjustments whenever they were needed. But they weren't people to me, they were resources. That's what the company wanted from me, to use the resources efficiently. The only way I knew how to do that, was to look at everything objectively.

It was unfortunate that none of my colleagues could understand that. Louise in particular often gave me a look of disdain when I announced decisions that would have an impact on the individual's life, but I dismissed her reaction as not relevant. The contracts of employment were worded so that it would be reasonable to make all sorts of changes and still be within the boundary of what they agreed to. Making changes that were allowed for, but unpopular, only rewarded me with more and more isolation. If it wasn't for Louise's sweet nature, I'd have had no one to say a kind word to me. After she'd heard about my relocation of Belinda down to the Cookware section, even she stopped making pleasantries.

It was bad timing that I had to report to the board on the very day that I'd got ready in a hurry. I'd slept badly for a few nights in a row and so I overslept, having switched my alarm off rather than to snooze again. I rushed into the office and noticed Louise giving me a strange look, but she turned away before I could ask her what the matter was. I gathered my reports and rushed into the meeting that had already started. There was a fairly new member there called Rob Johnson, a finance director, brought in to make more efficiencies and restore the company to the level of profit they'd enjoyed in the past. I stepped in and noticed a couple of them repress a smile as I stood there. I apologised for being late and sat down.

The rest of the day passed uneventfully and then Rob came in to the office as I was reviewing the holiday allocation charts. He asked me if things had got better for me throughout the day and I thought he just meant my lateness for the meeting. Then he pointed out that I was wearing one black and one navy blue shoe. Similar design, but definitely different. I blushed, thinking I couldn't remember the last time I'd felt so embarrassed. The mismatched shoes explained why Louise had given me a funny look and also some of the other board members. I sat back and sighed, finding myself telling him why no one had told me and how unpopular I was. He chuckled and said he was just the same. He'd not made a single decision that had been liked.

Rob and I met up for lunch regularly after that, enjoying the fact that we'd each found someone who was equally unpopular as ourselves. He'd just implemented an overtime ban, and I'd had to tell three apprentices that they wouldn't be offered further employment now that they were qualified. The more I talked to Rob, the more I realised that I wasn't really happy with my work and that I didn't want to be called the Ice-Queen behind my back. He said he felt the same and was particularly peeved that no one had told him he'd left his car lights on, despite half a dozen people parking after him. He said he was annoyed with himself too, because he'd put his headphones in to finish listening to a bit on the radio he was enjoying, so he didn't hear the warning beeps from the car. He'd had to get the RAC out to get him started when it was time to leave, as apparently no one had any jump leads either.

I knew Rob was married and so I made myself look at him only as a colleague, a welcome friend in a place that was otherwise hostile to me. I realised I'd brought my isolation on myself and wondered from time to time if I should try and change how I thought about the employees. But whenever I did make an effort to be kind to the workers, the company was much worse off, and I couldn't reconcile how to do my job. I only knew one way. It was then I decided I needed to leave. I wasn't fulfilled by work alone and I could see I was going to be a lonely old spinster resorting to taking in stray cats.

I was taken aback by Rob's reaction when I told him I'd handed in my notice. His face crumpled and I thought for a minute he was going to cry. He said how much he'd miss me and asked where I was going. I told him I was having a complete change of scene and was going to work in a coffee shop. He actually laughed and said he couldn't picture me making a cappuccino and serving up slices of cake. I told him I couldn't picture it either, but I didn't need a lot of money as the big mortgage was now very manageable, I just wanted a purpose. I was amazed how much I was actually looking forward to it.

When I'd been at Coffee At The Café for a month, I sat down for my break and took stock of what was happening to me. I no longer had any trouble sleeping and instead of sitting in silence most of the day with only a computer and sheets of figures for company, I chatted all day long with customers. I smiled more than I remember ever doing in my life. I knew I'd made the right decision, even when my first pay slip showed just how much less a Barista earns compared to an HR Manager. But the resources I was dealing with now didn't have feelings and I couldn't ruin their lives with a tough, but financially prudent decision.

And then the icing on the cake of my new, much happier life, was when Rob came in one afternoon. He sat around, drawing as many cups as he could from one teapot, happily waiting to chat to me in between me serving other customers. I thought he'd say he had to leave and we wouldn't have had much of a catch-up. But there he was at the end of the afternoon as I wiped down the tables. I sat with him and that's when he made his big announcement. He'd finally decided to leave his unhappy marriage and was already settled in the spare room of a friend of his. And therefore, would I go out to dinner with him? I told him I would and he was delighted until I gave him my stipulation. He had to leave Harper and Hughes as well. He was too surprised to give me a straight answer, so I sent him away to think about his life and what was important to him. But the philosophy of cost cutting at the expense of people, wasn't something I wanted to be associated with anymore, even indirectly through a boyfriend.

I'm hoping he'll leave there, for his sake as much as mine. And while I'm waiting, I've got the quiz night to go to with the rest of the girls from the café.

The iPhone's Fault *(Vicki's Tale)*

I love my iPhone. I'm never without it. I love all the apps, email, internet, games; oh and of course being able to talk to my friends. And it takes great photos. That's what came in really handy last week. It wasn't my phone though, it was Jayden's. Ours are identical, got them at the same time. Except his has a small crack across the top corner of the screen. I recognised it at Chloe's party, sitting on the kitchen top, plugged into the charger. The crack in the glass caught the light from all the down-lighters she had in the ceiling.

At first I thought it might *accidentally* fall into the sink and have a load of water poured over it, but I was very good and resisted the temptation. Even though the gorgeous Ben was at the party, checking me out every now and again, I couldn't stop thinking about the phone, just sitting there. And where was Jayden? Sitting between his two best mates on the sofa getting very pissed. I heard he was gutted that his new girlfriend Ellie had to work the late shift and couldn't come to the party. Ah, he missed her. Bless.

I don't have anything against Ellie. It wasn't her fault she was going out with a filthy, cheating liar. He'd apparently told her we weren't together anymore and that we'd broken up a month ago. When of course we didn't actually split up until I found out about her. We were in a nice restaurant at the time, Jayden and I, eating some very fancy stuff. I saw the message from her, pop up on his phone, while he'd gone to the gents. I ordered the most expensive drinks and pudding that there was on the menu and confronted him when he came back. He couldn't deny it. I walked out, leaving him to pay the massive bill.

So it's better for Ellie to find out now what he's really like before she does something stupid like falling in love with him or getting pregnant.

Everyone was dancing in the living room when Dancing Queen came on. Chloe was totally out of her tree, laughing her head off at the slightest thing. She started stripping everything off except her very skimpy red dress, which was far too tight over her big boobs.

That's what gave me the idea. I got Jayden's phone from the kitchen. No-one saw me. He was the one that showed me you could do this; take a photo without having to put the PIN number in. I knew he'd have changed the code as soon as we split up. I tried it just in case. After all, I could have even more fun sending some texts out. No, I was right, he had changed it. Still, I took some great shots of Chloe's cleavage and her flinging her head back, arms above her head. She looked really sexy like that. I made sure the kitchen was empty when I put it back. Now I could forget about it and enjoy the rest of the party.

I knew it would only be a matter of time before Ellie found them. Jayden loved to show off his photos. I'd seen the same sunsets and selfies, God knows how many times.

It happened after three days, but I'd have bet it being a week. So there it was, confirmed on Facebook. Jayden's status. Single. Result.

I don't feel the slightest bit guilty. It's those iPhone people that should feel bad, letting just anyone take photos on peoples' phones. And Jayden deserves everything he's got. Now he knows what it feels like to be dumped.

Oh, what's this? Ben wants me to join the quiz team tonight. You know what, I might just do that. These phones are great for looking up answers.

A Nice Slice of Cake *(Stan's Tale)*

We were lucky to spot two seats by the window, our favourite place in the tea-room. I hurried over to claim them, putting my coat over the back of one and my paperback on the other, whilst May hobbled behind me. Once she'd sat down, I went over to the counter and queued up with my tray. I got a pot of tea for us both and a shortbread biscuit for me. For May, I selected the largest of the slices of chocolate cake, knowing it was her favourite.

I said hello to Rowena behind the counter whilst she took my card payment and we had a little chat as we usually did, if there weren't any customers behind me. I always added on a tip.

May and I tucked into our afternoon treat in companionable silence. This summed up how we were with each other, companionable. We didn't ask for a lot from each other anymore. As I looked out of the window, seeing the way the sun was shining on the church, I was reminded of our wedding day. It was over thirty years ago now, in the local Catholic Church where we had met. It had been a slow start, us being pushed towards each other by well-meaning friends and family.

The more time we spent together, the more each of us became convinced we were a good match. As we both had strong faiths, we knew we were binding to each other for life. A divorce would never be an option.

I smiled at May and wiped a bit of chocolate fondant from the corner of her mouth, with my napkin.

'How's your biscuit?' she asked.

'Lovely, thanks. Your cake all right, not too dry?'

'Oh no, it's just right.' May took another big bite with obvious enjoyment.

I poured us out a second cup of tea and sat and watched Rowena bob back and forth round the tables. I was pleased she seemed happier these days. A few months ago, I'd caught her crying when she thought no one was looking. May was happy reading her magazine and so I sat and asked her what was wrong. She told me all about her boyfriend that had upped and left without a proper goodbye. She called him her boyfriend, but she was only a few years younger than me, so he was well past being a boy and far too old to break up with someone by text. I told her she deserved so much better and she seemed cheered by that.

May didn't talk to her much, mainly because she liked to sit down as soon as we arrived, as her knees gave her a lot of trouble now. As well as her hips.

Our wedding kept coming back into my mind and how we had just a few of our real friends and family there, but the usual congregation had attended and swelled the numbers. I only had my brother and cousin now, but May didn't have any family left anymore, they'd all dropped down dead from heart disease.

Only last night there was a programme on TV about the state of the nation's health and that too many of the population were obese. I suppose that's how you'd describe May. She went to see the doctor quite often, but she wouldn't let me go in with her, preferring me to stay with the car and have it parked close to the surgery entrance. I don't know if he gave her any advice about her weight, but if he did, she didn't seem to follow it.

We had regular things we did every day since I'd retired early and looked after May. We still went to Church on Sundays and I was pleased that we did. It was still an important part of our lives. I tried to live as I thought God wanted me to, but I sometimes felt as if I was being tested.

We'd planned to do the food shopping after our tea stop, but May said her right knee was really bad today.

'No news on when it might be your turn to get a replacement?' I asked, thinking it must have been two or even three years that she'd first said the doctor had told her that's what she needed.

'No, these waiting lists are enormous,' she answered, but didn't look straight at me.

Rowena was standing chatting to a customer, just a few steps away from May. I couldn't help look from one woman to the other. Not for the first time, I thought

Rowena's boyfriend must have been a complete idiot to have given her up.

'I don't really want to just go home.' May said, 'It's so nice just sitting here looking at the world going by.'

'Well I can do an online shop later. We can stay and have another pot of tea if you like.' I smiled at May.

'I'd like that.' She said.

Rowena was carrying a tray and coming in my direction, so I could see her at the same time as seeing May. I think the sight of them almost side by side, brought out a dark streak in me and I knew I'd have to go to confession soon.

'They've got some lovely looking carrot cake at the counter,' I said, 'would you like some? One of your five a day!'

'You are naughty, encouraging me like that, but go on then,' she giggled.

I smiled. If only she knew.

Acknowledgements

I have been writing for just over thirty years, having been on several Arvon Foundation courses, belonged to two writing groups and attended theatre writing lessons over many months. I've been lucky enough to have had some stories published in anthologies and for all fourteen of my full length murder mystery plays, to have been performed on the amateur stage as fundraisers. I was introduced to fundraising back when I was a teenager, joining Rotaract, and later Rotary and from those connections, have been able to see the plays come to life. My love of stories and reading started when I was a child, growing up with my brother Keith, with our mum and dad who showed us much love and kindness.

Having decided I wanted to put my favourite stories together in a collection, I asked for help from my friend Adrian Burroughs and my daughter Emma Tuohy. They helped sift through them and gave invaluable feedback as to what would and wouldn't work. Most importantly they gave me the confidence to bring two collections together, one for crime and the other about life's dramas, for which I am very grateful.

Throughout my adult life, I've been able to do so much writing, alongside working at an advice agency, thanks to the continued support from my dear husband Nigel Tuohy, who I am indebted to.

I would like to thank my long standing writing friends who have been a great encouragement for all my writing projects. They are Ruth McCracken and Penny Canvin. I'd also like to thank my beta readers for helping me make these stories the best they can be. I really appreciate all the support and time they've given me. They are fellow writers Sue Turbett, Steve Goodlad, plus my friends Adrian Burroughs and Jim Filer.

Thank you for choosing to read A Touch of Drama at Bedtime. I hope it didn't keep you awake.

Karen Banfield

Printed in Great Britain
by Amazon